What people are saying about …

Operation Bonnet

"*Operation Bonnet* has it all—romance, intrigue, and characters you'll fall in love with. Stuart masterfully weaves hilarity and heart. She will make you laugh, cry, and eagerly await her next release. This author is at the top of my favorites list."

Jenny B. Jones, award-winning author of *Save the Date* and the YA series A Charmed Life

What people are saying about …

Stretch Marks

"The novel to buy alongside *What to Expect When You're Expecting!* Funny, poignant, and cleverly written, Kimberly Stuart's *Stretch Marks* reminded me of all the misadventures, challenges, and joys of being pregnant—and the surprises that come with motherhood. A delightful read from an author who tells it like it is!"

Susan May Warren, award-winning author of *Nothing but Trouble*

"*Stretch Marks* is an absolute gem! Funny, authentic characters live out their messed-up lives and experience the deepest graces of life and spirit. Bravo, Kimberly Stuart!"

Ginger Garrett, author of *Chosen: The Lost Diaries of Queen Esther* and the Chronicles of the Scribe series

"What a sparkling, sassy—with the word twirled in gold sequins—hilarious, brave, and smart romantic comedy. The characters in *Stretch Marks* are so engaging I want to take yoga and color my hair with them! This is Kimberly Stuart at her finest, a soaring triumph for Christian fiction."

Claudia Mair Burney, author of *Zora and Nicky* and *Wounded*

What people are saying about …

Act Two

"Like fine music, fine novels entertain us with tempo, depth, and well-timed crescendos. In *Act Two,* Kimberly Stuart proves herself a deft composer. Bravo!"

Ray Blackston, author of *Flabbergasted*

"Order takeout, kick off your shoes, and turn off your phone: Kimberly Stuart delivers another sassy, funny novel with a high-strung heroine you'll love! Get ready to curl up with a laugh-out-loud book!"

Ginger Garrett, author of *Chosen: The Lost Diaries of Queen Esther* and *Beauty Secrets of the Bible*

"From the shimmering streets of Manhattan to the snow-covered fields of Iowa, *Act Two* delivers an entertaining and redeeming story about the power of second chances. Bravo!"

Anne Dayton and May Vanderbilt, authors of *The Book of Jane*

"*Act Two* is not just a novel with perfect pitch; there's a joyful grace note calling us to God on every page. Kim Stuart's most fun and stirring novel yet."

Claudia Mair Burney, author of *Zora and Nicky* and *Wounded*

Operation BONNET

a novel

KIMBERLY STUART

David C Cook
transforming lives together

OPERATION BONNET
Published by David C Cook
4050 Lee Vance View
Colorado Springs, CO 80918 U.S.A.

David C Cook Distribution Canada
55 Woodslee Avenue, Paris, Ontario, Canada N3L 3E5

David C Cook U.K., Kingsway Communications
Eastbourne, East Sussex BN23 6NT, England

David C Cook and the graphic circle C logo
are registered trademarks of Cook Communications Ministries.

This story is a work of fiction. All characters and events are the product of
the author's imagination. Any resemblance to any person, living or dead, is
coincidental. StraightTalkWithSergeantJack.com is a fictitious Web site imagined
by the author. As of this book's publication date, no such site existed.

LCCN 2010940548
ISBN 978-0-7814-4891-8
eISBN 978-1-4347-0328-6

The author is represented by MacGregor Literary.

The Team: Don Pape, Jamie Chavez, Amy Kiechlin, Caitlyn York, Karen Athen
Cover Design: FaceOut Studios, Tim Green
Cover Image: iStockphoto, royalty-free

Printed in the United States of America
First Edition 2011

1 2 3 4 5 6 7 8 9 10

112910

FOR MARC

1

This Little Light

I didn't set out to be the town luminary. True, there wasn't exactly a lot of competition in Casper. I nailed that down halfway through fifth grade with Mrs. Potts. She was an apple-shaped woman with a tight perm and cankles. I remember her as a round, fluttery circle, her hands fanning herself when excited, which was often, and her double chin quivering with joy when we started the unit on Important Literature. Now that I've read all Dickens's work, I find it a tidge insulting that she pretended we were reading the real *Great Expectations* instead of that condensed rot in our reading workbooks, sandwiched between poems about caterpillars and rainbows.

"Children." She rapped a few pudgy knuckles on the whiteboard for silence. Completely insulting, calling us children, even though Lyle Woodruff had just been sent to the office for accidentally sealing his lips with rubber cement. "Group work should not be this noisy."

My group that day was a threesome, a horrible mistake given the rules of adolescent friendship. One of the three is always a runt, and that day I was conspicuous in my social station. I remember staring at Misty Warren and Angela Hopkins, both of them well into their full-throttle journey toward uselessness. Misty paused in a detailed analysis of her own cuteness and narrowed her eyes in my direction. She scanned my side ponytail and freckles with a practiced disdain.

"What are you looking at, Orphan Annie?" She cocked her still-life Aqua Net bangs, eyes flashing.

Angela snickered, too hard, so it sounded like a snort. She turned nearly as red as Mrs. Potts, who had waddled over to our group.

"Young ladies, how are you finding Mr. Charles Dickens?"

Misty shrugged. "Boring."

Angela nodded gravely. "I don't get it."

Misty added, "Yeah, I mean, why can't we read what we *want* to read? Like the Sweet Valley High books?"

Angela snicker-snorted.

"You really should stop that," I said, staring the way my mother always said made her nervous. "I can hear the snot rumbling around in your nose."

Misty turned slowly to face me, as if just then, regrettably, she'd remembered I was there. She pulled her upper lip into a sneer and said, "You. Are. So. Disgusting."

I turned to Mrs. Potts. "I like the book." I pointed to the open Dickens on my desk. "Estella seems like an interesting character."

Mrs. Potts raised what was left of her overplucked brows. "How so, Nellie?"

I shrugged. "It looks like she's going to represent something. Maybe the conflict between rich and poor, or the irony of being beautiful but having nothing going on between the ears." I tapped my own head conspiratorially and nodded toward my group mates.

Angela and Misty slouched within their diminutive desks, chins tucked into their necks in indignation.

"Oooh, well, let's use building-up words," Mrs. Potts said, but her fluttery hand went back to work near her throat. She began to splotch. "Nellie, I must say, in all my years of teaching fifth grade, never has someone had such an excellent and *astute* literary analysis so early into our Dickens unit." The jowls were in full quiver now. "Frankly, I'm shocked. Impressed, that is. Delighted. You're quite the literary *luminary*."

I could feel she was waiting for my response to that word, which sounded pretty good but had not come up yet in my word-of-the-week flip calendar. So I shrugged, as if *luminary* was as frequently used in reference to Nellie Monroe as *weirdo*, *dork*, and *nut job*.

Misty Warren popped her gum to break the spell. Mrs. Potts dispatched her to the trash can at the front of the room, and Angela jumped up to shuffle alongside though she couldn't chew gum with braces and rubber bands.

Mrs. Potts patted me on the head as the bell rang for lunch. "Excellent work, Nellie."

A luminary, I thought as I picked up my Trapper Keeper. Later that year, I'd flip my calendar to the word *swagger*, which was precisely what I did on my way to the cafeteria.

Mrs. Potts might have admired my literary prowess, but she was conspicuous in her affection. Most people in town seemed confused by me (clergy), scared of me (teachers), or irritated by me (peer group). Misty Warren, for example, seemed perpetually annoyed whenever

I raised my hand in class, took a stab in the dark and smiled at her, or asked for a pinky dip into her Carmex. That last one sent her through the roof.

I had my theories on the reactions I brought out in folks. For one thing, people in Casper didn't know what to do with a person with two middle names. Provincial, I know. But Nellie Augusta Lourdes Monroe was just one too many names for them. I've had a few grandmothers in my day, and my name shows the wear and tear of that whole family drama. Grandma Nellie died long before I was born but grew up on an unyielding farm in Nebraska before marrying my sinfully wealthy grandfather. Nellie was known for a sharp tongue and flaky piecrusts. Such a shame which of those gifts my own mother inherited. Augusta was my paternal grandmother who smelled like cinnamon and Old Spice, her favored cologne because she believed it to prevent cold sores and bad breath. (I assure you she was incorrect on both counts, though it does attract mosquitoes.)

And Lourdes was just an afterthought tacked on during Mother's brief flirtation with Catholicism.

As a nod to my childhood demographic, I didn't even make people flip the *r* in Lourdes. They *should have* out of respect for the French and Mary and all that, but I knew to pick my battles around this town. Even without the French *r*, official ceremonies were always struggles. The pastor at my confirmation kept calling me Nellman Augusta Loor-deez, even though he'd known my family for years and even dated my mother in high school. When I got my driver's license, the woman at the counter burst into laughter when I pronounced Lourdes the correct way. I was rather offended, though I felt better when Pop assured me it was a great honor to get an Ohio BMV employee to laugh.

The only people who said my name correctly were Nona and Tank. Nona deserved extra kudos, as she was the one grandma I was not named after. She was the last in an impressive line of divorcée grandmas, lucky number four of the wives who endured my grandfather, Allistair Byrne. Alli, as I'll call him since I never had the pleasure of meeting his smarmy self, was quite the ladies' man. It helped that he inherited a pot of money from his own father, Casper's railroad tycoon and town miser, Seamus Byrne. Nona met Alli, married Alli, and was disdained by Alli all within the space of five years. Just after the divorce was final, however, Allistair clutched his heart during an otherwise uneventful board meeting, slumped in his maroon leather chair, and was gone. My mother, newly postpartum and burdened by grief, asked Nona to move into the Byrne estate with her and Pop and the new, colicky baby named Nellie. Mother's only explanation at the time was that Nona was "the only one that had been worth the Byrne name," presumably nixing her own mother and perhaps her father, too, though no one clarified. She was in mourning, after all. At any rate, Nona arrived with a trunk of clothes and a strong hug the next day and had never left.

So Nona knew how to say my name. And Tank, well, he was just about the only person who didn't irritate me over long stretches of time. This was the reason I continued to work for him at a ridiculous job with ridiculous people.

"Morning, Nellie," he called out when he heard the screen door slam that first day of the summer season.

"Good morning," I said as I fished out my time card from the slot and gave it a decisive stamp of entry. "First day of summer, Tank. How are you feeling?" I asked the question but could have lip-synched the answer.

"Eighteen holes to be CONQUERED, and all is well with the world."

Tank's response, the same every season opener for all the years I'd known him, reminded me of my high school phys-ed teacher, Ms. Stricken. An unfortunate name for a woman in her place of employment—a high school, the land of the unforgiving. Ms. Stricken was memorable for two reasons, neither of which had anything to do with my education under her wing: (a) her adult acne, another blow to the name issue, and (b) the joke she told every single first day of class. In total, I heard her gravel-voiced delivery eight times in four years. It never improved: "Wear gym shoes only, no black soles. Three tardies equal a detention with me in the wrestling room. I promise it will stink. And lastly, don't wear shirts with beer logos on them. Makes me thirsty, heh heh."

After decades of this pep talk, Ms. Stricken still taught at Casper Senior High. If I had any passion for children, which I didn't, I'd try getting her fired. But I had other aspirations, *serious* aspirations that had nothing to do with this sleepy town.

"Nellie? You listening to me?" Tank leaned over the front counter, poking his head down where I crouched on the floor folding a pile of chamois.

"Sorry, Tank. I was just thinking about high school." I continued stacking the towels but heard Tank sigh.

"Oh, man, were those great years or WHAT?" Tank tended to

raise his voice on words he deemed in need of emphasis. I'd seen it annoy people, but I kind of liked it, particularly when he yelped my name. It was an *affectionate* yelp.

"Your dad and I, that year we won state, good GRAVY, were we on top of the world." The sun-carved wrinkles around Tank's blue eyes framed an animated jog of his memory. "Last hole of the day, down by two strokes, and your dad had to putt. Nobody can PUTT like your dad." He shook his head, lost again in the glory of state championship golf, '77.

"I don't know about that, Tank," I said. "I've seen you dominate the green." Part of being a luminary is knowing how to speak other people's languages, even if it's something as inane as golf. Multilingualism isn't just about *el español,* people.

"Ah, NELLIE," he barked, slapping the counter. "Just one of the reasons I love ya, kid. You know how to build up an old man." He clapped me on the side of the head, a habit I'd tried in vain to break in him.

"Tank. The head." I pointed to my afro. "Please."

"Sorry, sorry," he said, striding toward the line of golf carts standing sentry outside. "What am I supposed to do, though? Hug you? I'm not a hugger. . . ." I heard him mutter to himself as the screen door slapped behind him.

In his defense, no one really knew how to respond to my hair. Perhaps slapping it was Tank's way of trying to tame it for me. For starters, I was definitely Anglo-American—three-quarters Irish and one-quarter Miscellaneous Pale, to be exact. That could throw a person straight off, because the wiry curls on my head weren't often seen on the kind of girl who burned to a crisp every single summer, beginning on Memorial Day and barreling right through Labor Day. Second, my hair was orange. Not auburn, not strawberry blonde, not russet or anything else out of an Emily Brontë novel. It was orange, and I'd come to peace with it. There were a few years in there when I let Mother drag me around to hair salons in the area, once even driving as far as Cleveland in an effort to straighten, dye, thin, or otherwise subdue the mop she was *sure* came from someone of dubious moral standing on my father's side. I was fairly positive the expenses incurred ran into the thousands, all of which would likely come out of my inheritance. Around about ninth grade, though, I put a stop to the whole charade and told my mother I was happy with my hair. I remember her literally choking on her biscotti, her eyes bugging as she said, "*Happy* with it? I don't understand." Not many do, I suppose, but I just didn't see any point in trying to make me look any different than I do. It'd be like trying to clear a patch of rainforest to plant a prissy English garden. Sometimes nature just keeps kicking back, in the jungle and with kinky Irish hair.

I twisted one strand around my finger and slapped it back with a bobby pin. I kept a plastic case of them next to the cash register for just that purpose. By three o'clock on a high humidity day, if I had nothing with which to rein it in, my hair extended to the size of a Thanksgiving platter all around my head. Men and women alike, filtering in after a hot round of eighteen, had been known to find the strength to gasp.

I was pulling out a fresh box of mini pencils and a stack of scorecards from the storcroom when I heard a human or large animal rustle behind me. I whirled around, screeching like a ninja, and slugged the rustler right in the gut.

"Aaargh!" I yelled again, even after I saw the rustler was a young guy in jeans and a T-shirt, doubled over and not looking particularly dangerous. Still, a girl needed always to establish the Alpha Dog in an attack situation.

"I am sorry I am late," he said, struggling to get a full breath. It really was a great punch. "The walk was longer than I thought." He looked up at me from his hunched position, and I could sense immediately that this was no predator. I wasn't sure he'd even started shaving.

"Are you hurt?" I helped him straighten up.

"No." He cleared his throat. "But you are a strong kind of woman."

I rolled my eyes. Flattery would get this kid nowhere. "You really shouldn't sneak up on people. I'd recommend speaking rather than skulking."

He looked at me. "Skulking?"

This was the kind of conversation common to a literary luminary. Always, *always* defining words. I was a walking, afro-ed dictionary.

"To move in a stealthy or furtive manner."

"Stealthy?"

See what I mean?

"Like you're hiding something."

"Ah," he said, nodding. "No, I don't hide things."

"Good to hear. Now, what can I do for you?"

He jumped when Tank came slamming back in the front door.

"You must be Amos." Tank charged for the boy, hand thrust out for a vigorous shake. "Glad you could GET here." Tank turned to me and winked very slowly, which is something no grown man should attempt. Could make a person think he's having a stroke.

"Nellie," he said slowly, "Amos here used to be AMISH, isn't that right?"

Amos nodded once and started scanning the room with a pair of enormous blue eyes.

Tank continued talking in his helpfully slow speech. I wondered if he thought Amos had also fallen out of a tree and needed to be spoken to in a might-be-a-few-coconuts-short voice. "He, like so many of his people, is very good at CARPENTRY. So I've asked him to help me fix up a little mini-golf course down by the koi pond."

"I see," I said, relieved to finally hear about The Project. Tank masterminded one every year. The koi arrived a few summers back, though the first two batches died unceremonious deaths due first to overfeeding and then to a chlorine incident. We also had the wind-energy experiment, which was shut down by the electric company, and last year's karaoke night, which would likely resurface down the road.

"Mini-golf, eh?" I said, watching the blond kid through the slits of my eyes. I'd been trying out that look lately to inspire intimidation in the interrogated. "You know a lot about mini-golf, Amos?"

"Absolutely, no, I do not." He shook his head. "Mr. Tank said he wrote the plans for me to make."

I rolled my eyes, disgusted by his honesty, so typical of people around here. "That's cool," I said by way of good-bye. I returned to my counter, hearing Tank enunciate his plan to Amos as they left through the back door.

2

Where the Heart Is

It's not that I didn't like honesty. Honesty has its place. It was just bad for business, and I'm not talking about golf. I worked at the course to help out Tank because I liked him and he'd acted as a surrogate father during the years Pop was working the tar out of his real-estate business. When summers ended my work at the golf course, I helped out at Casper's apple orchard, giving kids tours, making them try apple cider, asking them over and over not to bite into the apples before they paid for them. Even at home, I was on the clock, so to speak. Nona and I were permanent house sitters for Mother and Pop while they were away, which, with a sprawler of seven thousand square feet, was pretty much a full-time job without health benefits.

So I kept plenty busy. Add on to that the responsibilities of being the town luminary, and you had the ingredients many could use to cook up perfectly fulfilled lives. I had to sigh when I thought this, though, because I was made for something greater. Something full of intrigue, suspicion, and intellectual, mind-bending danger.

I was made to be a private investigator.

The trouble was, people in Casper were like that Amish kid. Just when you thought they were up to something interesting, they turned out to be lifeless as corpses, and not even the violently murdered kind. Honest, hard-working, boring—in short, a PI's worst nightmare. Of course, with only twenty-five thousand people in town, my chances for a bustling practice were already limited. Cleveland would be better. There were far more people there (2,088,291 by last count of the U.S. Census Bureau), and more people meant more crime. More crime meant a need for PI Nellie Augusta Lourdes Monroe, all four names on the business card, thank you very much. I was just waiting for the right time, for extenuating circumstances to clear up, and then I'd be on the first bus to Cleveland.

Actually, I'd drive. But the bus sounded much more definitive. There was a certain poetry there, as I'd think Mrs. Potts would agree.

In the meantime, I honed my skills. The eye-slitting was one technique I'd come to appreciate through Jack Knight, from StraightTalkWithSergeantJack.com. Jack, America's Foremost Private Investigation Expert, was a retired cop and PI, and though he hadn't given his specific whereabouts, I was certain he was from New York City. That kind of sophisticated criminal insight couldn't have been nurtured in the Midwest. Jack was turning out to be much more helpful than any of my college courses had been to date. After forcing myself to complete the general education requirements, I'd practically skipped into my first day of electives last semester. Finally, a real criminal science course—that first one titled "Intro to Crime." Well, let me just encourage you to never take that class. I flew through the paltry textbooks by the end of the first week and sat, dumbfounded, while the professor droned on for *three weeks* about the Supreme Court decision of *Miranda v. Arizona*. A few times, I tried guiding the class to a more interesting and relevant discussion. For example, I asked Professor Whitley (or Professor Nitwit, as I came to call him privately) to describe his most dangerous stakeout. Or if he had any comments about the constitutional conflict with phone surveillance. Or if he'd ever had to use a weapon on a perp. For each of these interactions, Prof. Nitwit had the same response: "Oh, now, let's not get ahead of ourselves! There will be plenty of time for that in the upper-level courses."

If Nitwit had ever actually handled a weapon, I would shave my head and dance the samba. I was pretty positive he was never even a cop. Campus security, nothing more, and I'd put money on it.

So to make up for the disappointment of formal education, this was to be the summer of independent study. I had found Jack's site and picked up some good resources from Amazon, the most promising of which was titled *Becoming a PI: Everything You Need to Know but Won't Hear in a Classroom*. And the third, most important component: I would need to test my capabilities, even in the crime-barren land of Casper.

This eye-slitting technique, for example, had sounded a bit juvenile when I first read about it, but despite my skepticism, I could already sense the difference in those to whom it was directed. I'd come dangerously close to getting my mailman to confess to mail fraud the day before, and he wasn't the only one shaken by the eyes. Maybe not that Amish kid, but those Amish were a little off anyway.

Another technique imperative to the successful PI, according to Jack, was the ability to sift through the subtleties and read body language. This was what came to mind when a middle-aged couple came into the clubhouse that first morning of the season.

"Whew, is it gonna be a cooker!" The man slid a crisp white ball cap off his head and fanned his receding hairline. *Body language assessment: uncomfortably warm, likely due to the weather and not to a fever.*

"Boy, I'll say," chirped the wife, around fifty, short, medium build, showing evidence of recent Botox. Her eyes were fairly animated, but her cheeks didn't seem to move much. *Assessment: suffering the effects of wealth and the pressure to remain young. Prime candidate for "cougar" activity; that is, preying on a younger man who fulfills her need to be viewed as attractive.* Textbook, really.

Her eyes lit on me. She made all the motions of lowering her voice—leaning in, winking, and looking over a Nancy Reagan–sized shoulder—but spoke in an entirely normal volume. "Dear, can you point me toward the little girls' room?"

Is there anything as irritating as a grown woman referring to herself as a little girl? I nodded toward the back of the pro shop, keeping an eye on the husband to watch for a similar irritation. Nothing. He seemed oblivious, creasing and recreasing a dollar bill to feed into our vending machine. Amos the Amish boy walked past the screen door, laden down with a shoulder-load of two-by-fours.

"I'm going to the restroom," the woman said to her husband, all the syrup gone from her voice. The shift in tone and posture perked my PI ears right up, and I pretended to organize receipts while I listened in. "Stick with the diet soda, Frank," she said and actually poked his belly. "And *don't* drive off without me again."

He sniffed.

Now, this could be my first case of the summer, I thought as she power walked to the bathroom. I watched the husband, finally successful at feeding the dollar into the machine. He sucked down a regular Dr. Pepper with the force of an anteater. Tension, definitely. Repression, possibly. He hadn't even looked in my direction, but that said much more about my hair than his marriage. She said he'd left her alone before, which meant he could have been meeting someone on the sly. Or he was merely trying to escape her belly-poking clutches. All in all, a very real possibility of discontent that could translate into a need for my services. I wrote down my cell number and was ready to slip it to the woman when she returned to the front and threw her arms around the man's neck.

"I'm sorry I told you to drink diet," she said into his collar.

"And I'm sorry I didn't listen to you," he said into hers.

They kissed, waved good-bye, and walked off, hand in hand, to their air-conditioned Lincoln Town Car and uneventful, happy marriage.

And the problem was, this was so typical. It was as if the people of Casper had forgotten to read the news. Fifty percent of marital unions everywhere else in the nation crumbled in divorce. In Casper, the rate was something like 23, which was nothing but infuriating to a person in my line of work.

People have *to be unhappier in Cleveland*, I thought as I turned on the ceiling fans. Misery couldn't be only the stuff of fairy tales.

"Nona! I'm coming up!"

We had this understanding that I needed to announce myself as I ascended the stairs to the third floor, a converted attic with dormered ceilings, wide windows, and wood floors. The attic was Nona's, and she had free reign and roam. Nona had become quite fond of nakedness, and while I appreciated that this was her right as a woman of eighty-some years, I didn't really want to see the groceries, wrinkly as they may have been.

"Hello, dear girl," she said as she opened the door at the top of the stairs. She was fully clothed in a splattered paint shirt and jeans rolled up into big cuffs. "How was work?"

I slumped into the hug she offered. "Life-draining."

"Oh, Nellie," she said, pulling back from her hug. "You're such a smart girl. Why don't you get a job that uses all your brilliance?"

I smiled. "Thanks for thinking I'm brilliant. Sure you're not just saying that because we're blood related? Kind of?"

Nona walked over to the bow of floor-to-ceiling windows on the far side of the room. She waved me to her and said, "Come look at my new one."

The canvas was large, nearly the size of Nona herself, and splashed with vibrant pools of color. Effusive circles of cherry red giggled from the painting, playing with smaller circles of white, all kinds of green, blue, a touch of black.

"I like it," I said, and I did.

"Me too. I want to work in more yellow, but overall, it makes me happy." She cocked her head, and I watched her bright eyes search the painting inch by inch. I knew, after many years of watching, many hours in this room, that she was not chiding herself internally for not having made something better. Nona wasn't into self-punishment. She once told me that she'd done enough of that during the first forty years of her life to last her forever and then some.

"Why do you paint, Nona?" I plopped down on the worn orange suede armchair she kept by the window for me. "Here you are, in your waning youth, slaving away over a blank canvas when you could be playing bridge or bingo or pinochle. Why do you do it?"

I'd asked so many times before, but I needed to hear her answer, particularly after another mind-crippling day at the golf course.

She tucked a strand of hair behind her ear and picked up a brush. "I do not appreciate the suggestion that I should play bingo. At the very least, I should be able to play Twister. At my age, I'm entitled to a bit of fun. But to answer your question"—she dabbed a big splotch of yellow as she spoke—"I paint first to honor the God who paints the sunsets and oceans and human hearts. And second, I paint so I don't get cranky like so many of the old people in this world."

My Nona really should have been a writer. She had a way with description that few master—certainly none of those writers who get their little paperbacks into airport kiosks. Painting oceans and human hearts? Better than Hallmark!

"A new kid started at work today," I said, twirling fringe from a throw pillow between my fingers. "He's Amish. Or he used to be. Isn't it once Amish, always Amish?"

"Oh, no, dear. If he's left his home, I'm afraid he's been cut off from his church, maybe even from his family." She put down her brush. "Kool-Aid?"

"No, thanks." Nona drank tea for years but decided recently she couldn't stand the stuff, so she'd taken up Kool-Aid instead.

Sometimes she went through the whole day with bluish teeth and a bright purple tongue. If Mother was home, it drove her insane, a gratifying by-product.

"I knew an Amish girl once. Her name was Rachel, and she had the loveliest high cheekbones." Nona came to sit across from me. She looked out the windows and sipped her drink. The late afternoon sun fell gently on her tendriled white hair, gathered as always in a messy bun at the back of her head. "I've often wondered what happened to her."

We sat in silence. I always thought it insufferably rude to interrupt an elderly person in the middle of a memory. There were quite a few files up there, if you know what I mean. Eighty-two years of living meant a lot of photos to flip through before you got to the right one. After a minute or so, she shook her head. "That girl was so sad. She told me once that leaving the Amish was the hardest thing she'd ever done but that staying would have wiped all the life out of her." She crossed her ankles delicately, a reminder of many years in polite society. "I was newly and painfully married at the time, so I understood exactly what she meant."

We sat as the sun dipped below the tree line and left behind it a baptism of orange, magenta, and farther up, indigo. The clouds had thinned out to long wisps of combed cotton, gathering stripes of sunset color and showing them off as they changed. After a cluster of quiet minutes, Nona startled in her chair and turned her gaze to me. "Nellie, forgive me! I have been so busy with my own thoughts I didn't see you there! How was your day, sweetheart? I want to hear all about it."

I smiled at her and felt my heart become full and heavy in my chest. I stood and kissed her on her forehead. "My day was great. Thank you for asking."

She smiled up at me, her eyes sparkling and clear. "Can you stay for some Kool-Aid? I want to show you what I've been working on."

"Not now," I said, walking to the door. "I'm afraid I'm too tired. But soon, Nona. I'll be back really soon."

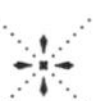

So you see, I couldn't go to Cleveland. Not on a bus or in a car, or on a boat or in a plane or any other way endorsed by Dr. Seuss. My Nona needed me, and I would be the scourge of humanity if I abandoned her. Scourge, from the Latin *corrigia*, meaning to whip: an instrument of punishment, cause of great affliction. No one a girl with four names, even a girl with her sights set on another life, could stand to be.

3

Tools of the Trade

I woke the next morning to the sound of wild turkeys hurling their fat, feathered bodies against the side of the house. I needed to squint at my *CSI* alarm clock for a full thirty seconds before making a plan to follow the airborne turkey noise to its origin. I kicked off the covers and padded over to my window. Kneeling on the window bench, I let my head rest on the cool glass. Down below, I saw the source of the flinging fowl sound: Mrs. H., our housekeeper and general drill sergeant for twenty-five years, stood neck deep in the hydrangea bushes, beating the tar out of a rug she'd hung over the porch rail. Mrs. H had to be nearing sixty, but she gripped a broom like a racket in the hands of that mannish tennis pro, Martina Complicated-Eastern-European-Name. I watched her without her knowledge, feeling just a big smug about being able to see her flap her arms and squat. Not the most flattering of poses for a woman who once told me a woman's dignity and a clean pair of underwear were all she needed in the world.

Despite her sketchy advice, Mrs. H. could take some credit for pushing me into the private investigating line of work. During the years I was growing up, she doubled as a nanny, monitoring me and my activities with the severity of a middle-school lunch lady. In between moments of bossing me around, Mrs. H. had a penchant for reading detective novels. After lunch each day, she'd clear and clean the dishes, set the kitchen right, and then sit down, with a long sigh, to read. Normal humans might have found a straight-backed wooden kitchen chair a strange choice for pleasure reading, but Mrs. H. was not a normal human. Mrs. H. thrived on discomfort, both personal and inflicted. There she'd sit, spine straight as a yogi's, reading Sue Grafton or Patricia Cornwell and pursing her lips in concentration. I once heard her gasp and looked over to see her clutching her heart. When she caught my eye, she said, "I *knew* he was the murderer." She shook her head, adding, "Never trust a man with an eye patch," by way of romantic counsel. I was probably twelve years old at the time. Watching Mrs. H., a normally unflappable personality, getting all riled up about justice and espionage and truth made me start wondering about the pull of a mystery to the human condition.

I turned away from the window and felt a small surge of gratitude toward her, all of which vanished when she threw open my door thirty minutes later.

"Nellie Monroe, what in God's earth are you doing?" She wrinkled her nose but still managed to look down it at me.

I let myself fall to the floor out of my handstand. "It would be really great if you would knock. Before entering. Now that I'm an adult."

"Pish posh," she said, picking up clothes off the floor and snapping them in the air. "Don't try to change the subject. For what good reason were you standing on your head?" Her cotton work dress buttoned all the way up, from a midcalf hem to just beneath her plump face. She *tsk*ed at the Coke stain on a pair of shorts, her neatly made-up face wrinkling at the moral failures all around her.

I sighed. "A headstand helps me focus. Changes the flow of blood in the body, restarts the old computer." I pointed to my head, which was sneakily buried underneath an eruption of morning hair.

Mrs. H. muttered to herself, rump in the air, as she straightened the shoes at the bottom of my closet.

"Hmm? What's that?" I said. I was allowed so few pleasures in my life. I worked at a par-three golf course with a man who shouted; I lived with my aging-though-beloved grandmother who routinely forgot to wear a bra; and I hadn't been kissed by a boy since senior prom, a moment that, I found out later, had involved the exchange of money. So can you cut me some slack if I liked to bait the woman who made me listen to Yanni every morning before school?

"Pardon me, Mrs. H. Did you have something to say to me?" I deliberately dropped one of the shirts she'd just folded to the floor.

"Oh, for the love of Peter, Paul, and Mary, Nellie! *Must* you create more work for me?" Mrs. H. buried her face in a pair of shoes she'd retrieved from the floor, then recoiled when she smelled them. She paused and pulled her spine up to her full height of five feet. "After you are finished doing your headstands and being generally disagreeable, you might take a moment to call That Friend of Yours. He's phoned four times in the last hour and is making it difficult to get anything done around here."

"Thanks for the message, Mrs. H.," I said, feeling just a tiny bit of regret for pushing all of her buttons at such a fragile hour. Mother always said I wasn't a morning person. "I'll call That Friend of Mine right now."

"Fine," she said, dropping a stack of folded shirts on the top of my dresser on her way out. "Tell him I don't say hello."

"I sure will." I'd picked up my phone and was already dialing.

"Finally." Matt must have been worked up. His voice almost had an inflection. "I've called about ten times. Didn't she give you the messages?"

"Mrs. H.? Of course she did. We Monroes, while certainly not faultless, do know how to hire and fire people. If Mrs. H. didn't relay phone messages well, she'd have been canned decades ago." I shimmied into the same pair of jeans I'd worn the day before and noticed they were a bit tighter than they'd been when I'd bought them. "I think I might be getting fat," I said, more bemused than irritated.

"Doubt it," Matt said, returned safely to his monotone. "Besides, you'd have to put on about three bills for anyone to see past the hair."

These are the comforts of old friendships. You can make fun of hair and not have that be the end of it. "Before I forget, Mrs. H. said to tell you she doesn't say hello."

"Ooooo, that's rough. I'll be sure to tell my dad when he gets home."

Mrs. H. and Matt's dad, Arthur DuPage, nursed a completely unhealthy grudge against each other for an unknown offense that occurred when they went to high school together. After much in-home espionage, document rummaging, and even the use of microfiche at the Casper Public Library, I still had no idea what happened. I tried prying some information out of Mrs. H.'s husband,

Mr. H., before he died ten years ago. To no avail. He was even more tight-lipped than she. He made his face blank, going so far as to let his jaw go slack. It was probably the closest I'd come to verifiable scandal in this town, and the H.'s shot the drama to bits. That I was friends with Arthur's son did cause Mrs. H. considerable angst, but most of what I got out of it was her reddened face, muttered curses every now and then, and the use of Matt's title, "That Friend of Yours."

"What's the rush, then? Why are you stalking me? People will start to talk." I picked at my hair with a wide-toothed comb but made no discernible progress.

"I'd actually be really great at stalking. You know—quiet, invisible type."

I know Matt better than most and could hear the small note of a smile in his words. "You should try that! Please, will you? Stalk someone, and let me be the one to get you on surveillance tapes so I can bust you and finally have a case under my belt. Please, Matt? Be a stalker for me?"

He cleared his throat. "Um, I don't think that would be a healthy boundary for us."

I rolled my eyes, glad he couldn't see. Ever since he'd started reading self-help on his way to a career in psychiatry, the man had the ability to stop friendly banter on a dime.

"The reason I called," he said, apparently pleased at our avoidance of crossed boundaries, "is that you should meet me at the store when it opens. You might be in the market for one of our hottest items, *which goes on sale today.*"

"Shut up. Are you serious?"

"As the grave. See you at ten."

One of the many perks of being friends with Matt, in addition to having a backup date to every school dance for grades seven through twelve, a person to sit around and be cynical with in college, and a person who didn't seem to tire of you even when you were stuck in a huge house with your grandmother and a cranky housekeeper, was that he worked at Radio Shack. A budding PI really needed a contact on the technological inside—someone who would, say, call with an alert that the recording device for which one had been pining was finally on sale and wouldn't cost a month's wages.

I gave up on my hair and pulled it into a horrible pink ball cap Mother and Pop brought me from Belize one year. I'd found the Radio Shack crowd to be less discerning in the ways of fashion than even I, the disappointing only daughter of Annette Monroe, fashionista of the universe and owner of sixty-four pairs of black high heels. I'd counted, and that number didn't include charcoal gray or prints.

"Nice hat," Matt said when I met him at the front entrance. "I didn't peg you to be one for pink." His voice never moved up or down one single note of the scale, but his dark eyes flickered with mischief.

"I have layers you haven't even seen," I said, looking past him into the store. "Let's go before they sell out."

Matt snickered. "I guarantee you will be the only one in Casper buying the Elite Xtra 680 Digital Voice Recorder today. You can probably not run."

Too late. I jogged through the aisles, waving quickly to Don, the store manager who looked disapprovingly at my speed. *Whatever*, I thought. I'd seen him sprint into a Cleveland Barnes & Noble the night the third Harry Potter book released. He was not one to cast stones.

When I got to the Elite, I picked it up and did a little dance in the aisle. I'd been waiting for this moment for four months, since the first time Matt had shown me the new model. My old recorder was too big, analog instead of digital, and far too obvious in the pocket of my jeans. I'd had to resort to wearing a trench coat on several occasions, which was entirely too Nancy Drew.

"Hello, Nellie." The voice was deep and familiar.

I turned. It was the Amish guy from work. He stood uncomfortably close to me and wore a neon green shirt with the words SPRING BREAK '98 on the front. I took a step back. "Oh, hi. Amos, right?" Part of PI work: steel-trap memory with names.

"Yes, I am Amos. How are you today?" He spoke with a slight accent, but very carefully. I got the feeling he was the kind of person who didn't much like making mistakes.

"I'm well, thank you." I showed him the Elite. "My Holy Grail is on sale."

"Holy Grail? I am here for a phone charger. Do I need a Holy Grail?" He began a perusal of the Elite display.

"Hey," Matt said, coming to stand by me. "Did you find one, or are we sold out?" He glanced at Amos and raised an eyebrow above his glasses.

"Amos, this is my friend Matt. Matt, Amos just started working at the course. He used to be Amish."

Matt let out a low whistle and put out his hand. "Wow. So you've probably not spent a whole lot of time in Radio Shack."

Amos's upper lip lifted up in a lopsided grin. "No, but I can shoe a horse in twenty minutes."

"Sweet," Matt said, nodding. He ran a hand through a head

of thick chestnut hair. Thick, but still comb-cooperative, the jerk. "Touché, my friend."

I was beginning to feel annoyed with the male bonding, so I made my move to go pay. "Nice seeing you, Amos."

"But wait, please. I want to know what is the Holy Grail." He smiled again. "You tell me about this thing, and I will teach you how to shoe the horse."

"I'm going to pass on the horses," I said, though Matt looked like he'd be in. "The Holy Grail is a voice recorder. I can use it to record conversations without anyone knowing." I couldn't help it: Saying the words aloud made me shiver.

Amos looked confused. "You don't want a person to know you are talking? Is this not impossible with your loud voice?"

He did not look embarrassed by the comment, and Matt looked delighted.

I sighed. "I *mean,* I can record the sound of my conversation, the audio."

Blank stare.

"Tape it? Have a copy of it later? Like a CD? Or a record album?"

Total confusion.

Matt tried. "Dude, like a podcast."

"Oh, yes, a podcast!" Amos's eyes lit up. "I love the podcast of Howard Stern! You can make a podcast like his!"

"Good gravy," I said under my breath. Who *was* this kid? "Right, kind of like that." Then, feeling the need to distance myself from Howard, I said, "It's for my work. I'm a private investigator."

Amos's eyes widened. "Oh, that is a very important job. I know about this job." He nodded sagely. "I have seen this many times on the show *Magnum, P.I.* with Tom Selleck."

I was fairly sure Tom Selleck was dead or perhaps in a home, but I let it go. "Exactly. It's very exciting, rewarding work." I shrugged. "I keep my job at Tank's as a diversion."

Matt coughed, and I threw him a dagger look.

"Well, it's good to chat with you, Amos," I said, walking backward toward the front of the store. "See you Monday."

He waved, unsmiling, not unlike a kid during his fifteenth revolution on a Ferris wheel. "Good-bye, Nellie and Matt. I hope you catch lots of bad men."

"Nice guy," Matt said as we left the store. He dug his hands into the front pockets of his jeans. "A little intense, but nice. Do you think he'd really show me how to shoe a horse?"

I shook my head, busy unwrapping the Elite. "Probably. Let me know, and I'll come record you yelping in pain when the horse lands you one in the kisser." I pushed the red button and recorded our entire conversation on the way home.

4

Comfort Food

I heard the laugh before I could see her. It was really more of a whinny than a laugh, so I couldn't take any credit for aural stealth. My location, the meat counter at TasteWay Supermarket, was at least forty feet from the front of the store, but I could hear her up at checkout. Misty Warren. Remember? Not the snorter but the insulter? She still lived in Casper and, unfortunately, ruined nine out of ten expeditions to the grocery store because she'd married into ownership.

When Bill, the meat guy who liked to floss his teeth behind the counter, handed me the filets, I took my time strolling along the back of the store. I was finished shopping for dinner and really didn't feel like lingering by the condiments, but neither did I feel like having to converse with Misty Warren. She was hyphenated now: Misty Warren-Pitz. That was seriously her new last name. I heard her using it as I dragged my feet toward the register.

"Misty Warren-Pitz," she said, holding out a clump of painted fingernails to a customer in line. "P-i-t-z."

I'd heard this before too. She spelled it out, as if the *z* canceled out the fact that everyone could only think about armpits. I started unloading my groceries and tried to remain inconspicuous, a skill I'd basically perfected in my research.

"Hey, there, Nellie," Mr. Lockhart said. He ran my filets, the bacon, and the shallots down the conveyer belt. "How's things?"

"Fine," I said in a small voice, keeping my eyes on the cash register. I wasn't afraid of Misty Warren, but there were times when I just couldn't muster up the strength to *endure* her. That afternoon was one of those times. My parents had just called to let me and Nona know they'd be home for dinner, and would I rustle up something homey and midwestern? My mother and father could have hired anyone at any time to cook anything, but I always balked at the idea when it came up because I enjoyed cooking. It was not something I advertised, because in a town like Casper, you might as well start hanging out in the church basement on permanent potluck duty. Not to mention what it could do to your social life, everyone all frantic trying to get you married off to some man who needed a woman to "make a house a home." People here still talk like that, and it made me want to hole up with Nona and take a vow of chastity, that's what.

I almost made it out of the store. The kiss of death came when Mr. Lockhart called after me, just before I reached the automatic sliding doors to freedom.

"Nellie, tell your dad I shot three under par last week! Probably not anything special for him, but I took home steaks that night for Irma."

I kept walking and waved without turning around, but it was too little too late.

"Excuse me," I heard her say. "Nellie Monroe? Is that you?"

I rolled my eyes before turning around, although she might have seen the conclusion of the arc as I came to face her. "Hi, Misty."

She put one hand on her hip and sighed dramatically. Exactly like high school, only without the orange-and-blue cheerleader's skirt. "It is so *hot* outside. Can you believe how hot this is for June?" She let her chin drop at the injustice of it.

"Yep. Pretty hot. Well, I better run." I turned to go.

"Nellie, with that hair, you would just be *stunning* in Forest Haven."

Misty sold berets. This was the newest incarnation in a long line of mercenary tragedies. First came the classics: Tupperware, Mary Kay, Pampered Chef. When I thought really hard, I could understand the pull, at least with Pampered Chef. Nothing wrong with providing the community with a few more stoneware pans and lemon zesters, all in the name of a woman building a career. But Misty seemed to have something of a retail ADD, as she'd hopped from five or six home-based businesses since then. We're talking lawn ornaments (predominantly gnomes); photo frames made entirely of recycled milk cartons; an exercise machine called Tush-B-Little, Tush-B-Quick (absolutely a real product; I got suckered into attending one of those parties and couldn't walk for three days); and my personal favorite, bras that pushed up and out with such force, victims sent Misty chiropractic invoices for months afterward. The newest in the long line of terror was berets.

"You think?" I asked and wished I hadn't.

"Oh, definitely," she said. "We should totally schedule a party! The hostess gets a buttload of free stuff."

Do you see why this would never work? Who wants to buy things, really, from a woman who employs the word *buttload* in a sales pitch?

"Thanks, Misty, but I'll have to pass. Talk with you later," I said, backing up and out of the store. When I stood at my car, rummaging in my bag for my keys, I noticed a tinge of pity for the girl. I may have been living in my parents' house and getting ready to cook them dinner, but at least I wasn't selling berets. Hope remained.

At the risk of sounding full of conceit, my parents' kitchen would have been a mausoleum were it not for me. My mother loved to tell a story at cocktail parties of the first and only meal she prepared as a young bride. It was not a very interesting story, but like all things my mother touched, it became more so with each retelling and a lot of hand gestures. The fated dinner involved a Cornish hen with a carcinogenic char, bread that remained disheartened and gooey on the inside, and mix brownies that made Pop ill. The consolation dinner after all that went awry was toast, which she burned. At this point in the story, Annette admirers would laugh with appreciation, saying things like, "What a great story!" and "It's a good thing you do everything else so well!" They, of course, didn't have to suffer in the home where burned toast was the *better* of two choices.

Even though Mother renovated the kitchen with all high-end, high-dollar finishes, she had yet to actually use any of them, with the exception of the automatic garbage can and the temperature-controlled wine drawer. There was a deep-fat fryer concealed neatly with a stainless-steel cover. I'd long ago earned the right to use the six-burner gas stove, the built-in griddle, the warming drawer. The subzero freezer was stocked with homemade chicken stock, filled pastas, cookies, my famous chocolate sorbet. All of this remained a secret to anyone outside the family other than Matt, who dubbed me Betty Crocker with a Sneer until I made him dinner. Then I swore him to unwavering secrecy and stoked that flame every now and then with baked goods. It was pathetic how quickly his allegiance firmed in the face of a chocolate scone.

I filled a stockpot with water to boil the new potatoes. The key to off-the-charts mashed potatoes is buttermilk. That and some healthy-sized crumbles of Maytag blue cheese. And butter. All things that might have adverse effects on your jeans fitting if you didn't keep in shape for the occasional high-speed chase.

I was trimming the asparagus when Pop appeared in the kitchen doorway.

"Hi, pumpkin," he said.

I wiped my hands quickly on my apron and rushed over to hug him.

"Ah, nothing better," he said, moving back to get a look at me. Following sun year-round gave my father a perma-tan, though Annette was careful to help him walk the line between a healthy glow and the George Hamilton syndrome. "A welcome-home greeting from my little girl."

"Right, except I'm almost thirty."

"What?" Pop looked panicked. "When's your birthday? September, right?"

I laughed. "Pop, I'm not really thirty. But I'm almost twenty-one."

"Oh, give me a break, Nellie." He sounded relieved. "You have nine years. At my age, nine years is the difference between a meaningless bump on your shoulder and a pine box."

"Wow," I said. "So much to look forward to. Have you been hanging out with the Olafsons again?" Stan and Rita Olafson were two little birds who looked more like brother and sister than husband and wife. They shared my parents' love of the PGA Tour, travel, and a good waitstaff, but they also infected Pop with a fear of mortality. I always knew he'd been with one of them when he'd ask me to take a look at his eyeball or his foot or his earlobe. He'd wait with expectation and then blurt out, "Well? Don't you see it?" I never did, but he never quit asking.

"As a matter of fact, I have." His voice came from deep within the pantry, right before he emerged with a bag of pistachios. "We were just talking about you on the flight home. Myles is still single, you know." He raised his eyebrows and crunched into a nut.

"I'm sure he is," I said. "I'm sure I am too. Yet I am *still* not interested in dating a person who sniffed Wite-Out during American civics in sixth grade."

Pop groaned. "Nellie, how about giving the guy a break? Must you punish him for the rest of his life just because of who he was in junior high?"

"Probably," I said, preoccupied with arranging a line of asparagus on a cookie sheet. I drizzled olive oil over the spears and tried switching the subject. "How was your trip? You look good, Pop." It was a sneaky diversion but true nonetheless. My parents spent a lot of time touring the world's endless offering of golf courses, most of them prohibitively expensive to people who couldn't list a yacht as a deductible business expense. Mother's money was nearly as old as the town of Casper. Great-grandfather Seamus, the railroad man, built the original footprint of the home we inhabited. Unfortunately, Seamus thought generosity was a character flaw and took great pride in keeping every dime to himself. I heard once that he required his wife to keep a ledger of what she ate so that he could withhold it from her monthly allowance. Sounds dreamy, doesn't he? And my parents wondered why I wasn't jumping at the chance to marry Myles Olafson. I'd keep my own ledgers, thank you.

"Great trip, great trip." Pop had opened a ginger ale and sat on one of the bar stools at the center island. He wore, as he had every day since the one on which he'd sold his real-estate firm, a collared and pressed golf shirt, khakis, and breathtakingly expensive shoes. There were variations on this theme. That day, for example, he'd chosen green and white stripes for the shirt and some sort of canvas boat shoe with leather accents. The shoes were really quite horrible, a cross of tastes between Edward Scissorhands and Arnold Palmer. Worse, they had likely cost the price of a round-trip ticket to Borneo. He wiped at the beads of water sweating off a bottle and onto the marble. "Perfect weather again in North Carolina, nice new course in South Carolina, fun stop in Charleston to see some of your mother's old sorority chums." He paused. "Wish you'd been there, pumpkin. Why don't you come along next time?"

I finished wrapping thick slices of hickory-smoked bacon around the pink fillets. "Thanks, Pop, but I have my job. Plus, Nona needs me."

The lines around his mouth deepened. "How is she?"

My eyes stung a bit, but it might have been because I was slicing shallots. "She's all right," I said, willing my voice to be cheerier than I felt. My pop didn't do well with crises, but it wouldn't have mattered if he had. There wasn't anything left for anyone to do.

"Well," he said, pushing back on the bar stool, "we sure appreciate you keeping her company when we're away." He swallowed and cleared his throat. The noise was abrupt, echoing off the tile walls. "I'd better tell your mother that dinner's in the works. Thanks for cooking, sweetheart." He came to kiss me on the cheek. "You make it good to be home."

I smiled, eyes still stinging. Shallots were typically milder than onions, but I might have bought a bitter batch.

5

Thicker Than Water

"Mmmm," Nona murmured at dinner that night, tucking a corner of her linen napkin into the crease of her smile. "Such a lovely thing, beef."

"You know," Pop said around a bite of asparagus, "you're an awfully good chef, Nellie. Must have gotten that from my side of the family." He winked at me and turned a playful glance on my mother.

"Hmph," she muttered, slouching a bit in her chair but mopping up every part of the red wine–shallot sauce that her slice of artisan bread would allow. I watched her. My mother was fifty-six years old, and she was smokin'. That was just the truth, one that I'd learned to accept long ago, most painfully in junior high. My male classmates would stare when she dropped me off before school, gangly arms and legs stopped midstride in games of pick-up basketball or Frisbee. Annette's lips were full and often painted in colors that would make me look like I worked in a saloon. Her body was lithe and sculpted, some from the hand of a capable surgeon in Cleveland, but mostly from her religious commitment to working out. My body, though technically slim, had benefited from little or no attention in the way of Pilates classes or aerobic exercise. And though eventually I learned to pluck my unibrow, I never did catch Mother's giddy excitement in her approach to the Lancôme counter.

Annette-Nellie joint appearances, then, built within me a quirky emotional fortitude. I spent many hours wondering aloud with Nona how it was, exactly, that the woman who could give Sophia Loren a run for her *lira* had spawned me, the girl who broke an ankle the *one time* in junior high she wore pumps instead of Chuck Taylors. With enough repetition, I became adept at hearing Nona's soundtrack in my head, the one that told me I was more than a girl with scary hair, more than a person who thought tweezers and razors were overrated. People still stopped and stared when Mother and I would shop together, her in knee-high Italian leather boots and me in Rockports. But with time, I tolerated others' shock that Annette and I were mother and daughter, and even felt less impact from the shock waves myself.

"How are things around here?" Annette said and took a delicate sip of water. "Did you miss us?" Her hair fell in soft and deceptively simple layering around her face, slightly shorter in back to fall in a frame around her jaw line. She fingered a sapphire pendant hanging around her neck. The jewel was held in place by a swirl of platinum, and her garnet nail polish reflected the light from the chandelier.

"We certainly did," Nona said. Her exuberance sounded too eager. "Nellie takes such good care of me." She waited and then kicked me under the table.

"Ow-ie-yesss. Nona and I did just fine. Nona in particular did fine. Probably finer than most people in her age bracket."

My parents stared at me, and I could see Nona bite her lip. It was my responsibility to keep Mother and Pop placated and happy so that they wouldn't bring up putting Nona away at Fair Meadows. Nona knew she wasn't herself, but she and I had decided a trip to the Meadows would be only one small notch up from shoving her off the dock down by the river. Nona was great, I was great, everything was peaches.

After a beat, Pop cleared his throat. "Good. That's good to hear. How are things at work? How is Tank these days?"

I put down my fork, plate cleared of everything edible, and suppressed a burp into my mouth. Mother frowned. I reported, "With the help of an ex-Amish kid, Tank is constructing a mini-golf course."

"Good grief," Pop muttered.

Mother shook her head. "Certainly you aren't surprised, Clive. Remember where you are." Returning was always rough on Mother. After weeks in five-star hotels, lunch dates at art museums, leisurely rounds of golf, socializing with people who shunned commercial air travel—the return to itty-bitty Casper, Ohio, wore on her. She'd grown up here against the force of her will and a fierce wanderlust. Mini-golf was just one more punishing metaphor.

"Nellie, honey, you know you're welcome to quit that job whenever you'd like," Pop said as he buttered the last slice of bread. "Don't wait until you're old like me to enjoy life." He shook his head. "When I think of all the years I spent working until I fell into bed at night...." Pop wouldn't have had to work a day after he married Mother, so deep were the reserves. It always made me stand up straighter when I could tell people he owned his own business and was very good at it. He'd missed every single Saturday and Sunday through most of my childhood, showing houses and negotiating offers. I had made him pay with my fair share of teenage whining and general snottiness. But the way I now saw it, all that time away had nudged me toward a great friendship with Tank, and I knew Pop loved me.

Can you believe how well-adjusted I was, and without a single visit to the therapist? I should write a book.

Pop picked up his knife, pointing it in my direction. "Why don't you tell Tank you're off to see the world? Take a few months in Europe. Or Africa."

"Greece," Mother said, her eyes lighting. "Greece is sublime. And the style there is very casual, Nellie. You'd be just fine."

I know what you're thinking. Here's a girl who was young, single, almost college-educated, brilliant, and reasonably attractive. Add to this a nice inheritance and the perpetual encouragement of her father to quit her low-paying job and kick back on a cruise ship or a tour bus or a safari Jeep before facing the perils of adulthood—if you think I was loony, you won't be the first or the last. I watched Nona's face cloud over. She ducked her chin, suddenly absorbed with her fork.

"I'm not really into feta and kalamata olives. Or falafel." I saw Nona smile at her plate. "Plus, I've finished my third online course in PI licensure. I can't leave now, when I'll probably be signing up lots of clients."

"Here we go," Pop said under his breath.

"Nellie, you cannot still be thinking of doing that," Mother said, pouring the last of the Shiraz into her glass. "I thought you'd given up by now." She clenched her jaw.

I clenched right back. I may not have gotten the lips, but I did get her spine. "I'll be really good at it. I just need to get my name out."

Pop cleared his throat. "Pumpkin, what's the salary for something like that? What does a PI make? An hourly? And what about benefits?"

"And what about that it's"—Mother hesitated, but the wine allowed her to plow right ahead—"it's trashy? Trashy work following around trashy people and learning about their trashy lives. It's unbecoming to a Byrne. *Or* a Monroe."

At this point, my hair and face were the same spot on the color wheel. I tried breathing deeply, and when that didn't work, I kicked the heavy upholstered chair behind me as I stood. I walked to the wall and vaulted into a headstand.

"What—Nellie, what on earth?" Poor Pop. He had never known what to do around so much estrogen.

"This helps me clear my head and relax. I need to think, and I'm not finished with this conversation." I closed my eyes.

"I will never understand you," Mother said, pushing back from the table and teetering just slightly on her four-inch heels. "You could have such a lovely life, even if you chose to work. National Merit Scholar, summa cum laude, swooning teachers all through school. And yet you are content to work at a golf course and take computer classes about private investigation." She shook her head. "I don't get it, Nellie. And frankly, it can be embarrassing when it comes up at dinner parties."

I could feel my feet falling asleep, high above me, but I stayed upside down. Even from my compromised vantage point, I could see Nona's frown.

"And," Mother continued, "people here don't even need a private investigator. You're wasting your life." Her last words sounded desperate. I was shocked to see her eyes shining with tears. Annette was known for lots of things, but public displays of sadness were not one of them. I remembered her shedding a total of 2.75 tears at the funeral of her great-aunt, but that was it for my entire childhood. I head-stood motionless, waiting to see if any tears would make the full leap over her lashes and onto the cheeks.

"Put your feet down," she said sharply. "Your soles are scuffing the walls." With that, she turned on one stiletto and walked out of the room.

"She almost cried," Nona said, awe filling her voice.

I let my legs fall forward and felt the blood rush back to its regular circulatory pattern. Pop sighed and said something about playing Tank's course before nightfall. Nona and I were left alone. She shrugged, smiled at me, and cut a ladylike incision into her cold steak.

6

Hired Hand

My first job found me that night. *It was dark, 2300 hours, a fog descending on the city....* I self-narrated all of this many times over the days that followed, and I must say, it was hugely satisfying. The fog part was the most delicious of the details, if something of a stretch. After the headstand conversation, I'd stepped outside for a walk. The air felt like a bully, humid and thick, even in the first part of June. When I passed under streetlights, I could almost *see* the air underneath, a summertime *fog* of sorts.

Honestly, I still might pursue fiction writing. Sometimes the words just flow.

The conversation at dinner had riled me. It wasn't really the things Mother had said. In fact, the topic was tired. I didn't expect anyone to understand why I was lured to a life of espionage, adventure, and danger. Misty Warren-Pitz would never understand a luminary, Mother couldn't understand a girl who wouldn't use an eyelash curler, and Pop couldn't understand the pull of twenty-four-hour surveillance. I was destined to live the life of an outsider, a nomad, a renegade. *Pariah* would be another great choice and was one of my favorite AP English words (Indian derivative, for one who is hated, distrusted), but that seemed a tad strong for Casper.

It wasn't being misunderstood that had rankled me. It was the feeling I needed to do something, fast. I needed to put all those Internet courses to the test, Cleveland be darned. There my mother sat, uncharacteristically emotional, almost crying, for glory's sake. She sat in her gigantic house, surrounded by horrible crystal figurines and fake eggs that cost more than the gross national product of Uruguay, and *still* she was unhappy. If Mother, in her perfect life, wasn't so perfect, there had to be more people like her right there in Casper. With enough years of imperfect living came desperation, and with desperation, money laundering, tax evasion, and eventually the Mafia. Maybe Casper wasn't the wasteland barren of indecent behavior I thought it was. Maybe I merely needed to look harder.

At the corner of Sycamore and Taylor, I paused, filling my lungs with the impossible air of a midwestern summer. I turned on Sycamore, heading to the elementary school playground for a swing, and heard the sound of footsteps not far behind me.

I froze, my heart racing. This was it. This was the moment I could finally justify all the hours of training, all the articles read, all the Bond movies committed to memory. I was formulating a very complicated yet effective plan when I felt someone's breath on my neck.

"WAAAAAAAAEEEE!" I screamed, sounding every bit the girl I was. It was a defeating picture, to be sure. But breath on the neck was not something covered in the online tutorial.

"It is I again!"

"Amos! You stealthy Amish freak!" I began hitting him with both fists, full bore and nothing like a weak-wristed girl. The adrenaline he'd spiked in me coursed through my body, making my arms and legs quiver like Jell-O. I kept punching until I heard a whimper. Arms at my sides, I finally stood still in the middle of the sidewalk, panting.

"You," he gasped, "are not hitting like a regular female. Or maybe this is regular for English girls?" He blotted a bloody lip on the hem of his shirt. Even in the semidarkness, I could see it was DayGlo tangerine.

I sighed. "Sorry. Again. But you really have to learn to announce your presence. I mean, sheesh, Amos." I was still shaken and took the opportunity to wag a finger in his face. "You try that anywhere else, like Dayton or Cleveland, and you'll get yourself shot."

His eyes grew big. "With a firearm."

"That's right," I said. "Like a Derringer or a forty-five." A breeze lifted the leaves in the trees above us, and I shuddered, my skin receptive and eager after fear-induced sweat.

"I am the most sorry," Amos said, his voice grave. "I would never want to scare any woman or be the cause of urban violence."

"It's okay," I said. I turned, and he rushed to join me. "As for the way I fight, you're right that most girls don't punch like I do. Most girls haven't undergone the training I have."

"I see." As we moved, his strides lengthened until I was nearly jogging to keep up. Still bruised from my sissy scream, I matched his pace and vowed to do so at the expense of aching quads. He walked, and I adhered to him like a terrier for three blocks before Amos spoke.

"I am looking to hire a Magnum PI."

I stopped and turned. It took him a few more strides to realize I wasn't beside him anymore.

Clearing my throat, I looked up, then down the street. "You have need for my services?" I raised one eyebrow and crossed my arms across my chest. No need to act overeager.

"Yes," he said, his voice barely above a whisper. "I understand if you are not in agreement with me. But please, first listen to my story."

I paused, appearing to mentally sift through my packed schedule, all the cheating husbands needing to be caught, the identity thieves needing a trip up the river, the long-lost war buddies hoping to be reunited. After a moment of contemplation, I relented. "All right," I said. "Let's talk."

I led him to the playground, each of us taking one of the wide black swings newly relieved to summer vacation. A pair of crickets sang an off-key duet to each other somewhere near the spiral slide.

I slipped the Elite from my jeans pocket and looked up. "You don't mind, do you?" I asked, gesturing to the recorder.

"No, of course I do not," he said. A lone lightning bug dipped lazily near Amos's crop of blond hair.

Ohyesohyesohyesohyes, I thought, my fingers shaking as I pushed the power button. *I'm using my Elite! For official business!* The thought of Matt's guaranteed awe flickered through my mind, but I got a grip and sobered myself for the work.

I cleared my throat and started the recorder. "Tenth of June, 2320 hours. Recreational equipment at undisclosed learning facility, air temperature approximately eighty degrees Fahrenheit, ninety percent humidity."

I could feel Amos's eyes on me. I gathered my hair and bunched it over one shoulder, grateful for the breeze that cooled my neck. "Client A will tell his story."

I nodded at Amos, but he sat, staring at the flashing red light on the Elite. After a few seconds of this, I pushed pause. "Are you ready?"

He dragged his eyes away from my hands. "Yes, I am ready. But"—he hesitated, shutting his eyes—"is it fine to put off the machine? I do not want to talk about her with a machine."

All those dollars, even on-sale ones, for naught. No matter, I consoled myself. There would be the chance to record a debriefing on my solitary walk home.

"Absolutely," I said, throwing in a sunny-natured shoulder pat for good measure. "Whatever makes you feel comfortable."

"OK. Good," he said. He dug his PUMAs into the pebbles under our feet and pushed off to swing. "I will tell you now why I, a man, need to pay you, a girl, to work privately for me."

There were better ways to word that proposition, but we could cover that later.

"I grew up on a farm forty miles in distance from here. Oh—" He stopped. "I was Amish."

"Right," I said. Perhaps he thought the tangerine shirt was a really effective decoy.

"On this farm, I was happy as a child. We raised potatoes and squash and corn and tomatoes and many other things to feed our family, having eight people. My father taught me how to drive our buggy, fix a horseshoe, build the barns."

I thought I saw Amos flex his pectoral muscles at the memory.

The action made me blush, which, in turn, made me irritated. I was working here, and no sort of Mrs. H. prudery could become a distraction.

"When I had twelve years old, I began to change."

I so hoped he didn't know the word for *puberty*.

"I was tall and strong for my age, so my parents sent me alone to town to sell our food. The farmers' market, grocery stores, even schools in the town—everyone liked to pay us money for our produce. No one grew any better." He stopped and swung in a small pendulum's arc, back and forth, back and forth. "I can taste the tomatoes when I think of them."

I watched his face, his mouth lopsided in a sad smile.

"So," I said, "you were twelve." I didn't mean to be insensitive, but it was inching toward midnight, and we had a good ten years to cover in Amos's story. After all those adrenaline rushes, I was starting to feel drowsy.

"I was twelve," he agreed. "This was the age when I knew I was going to be different. It is difficult to say the words." He bit his lower lip. "I love my family, but I am not like my family."

"Say no more." I nodded. "I know exactly what you're talking about, brother."

His brow furrowed. "I do not know you had a brother. Does he like that you are talking with a strange man in the darkness?"

I couldn't help it. I laughed. "No brother. I just meant my family doesn't understand me either."

"Ah," he said, nodding. "Did they shun you?"

Luminaries know the meaning of the verb *to shun* and don't like the sound of it. "Do they avoid me deliberately and habitually?" I actually had to think of my answer. "Technically, yes, but it's mostly because I won't go golfing with them."

Amos looked utterly lost.

"But this isn't about me. You knew you weren't like your family."

"That is right," he said. "I knew for many years before I left that I could not be Amish for my life. It is not in me." He pushed on his heart with his fist, so hard I worried he'd hurt those pecs. "I tried leaving three times before I stayed out. My returning was much suffering for my family, perhaps more than my leaving. I had to return, though. Because of *her.*" He stared at me in the darkness. I could see his eyes shining. "Katie."

A secret love interest, I thought. *This is the best day of my life.* "You love her," I said, watching his face in the lamplight.

He nodded, every bit as miserable as any Shakespearean hero. I got goose bumps just thinking about it.

"I do love her, but this was impossible." He got up off the swing and began to pace in front of me. Pacing, I knew from my online body language course, indicated discontent, restlessness, possibly rage. I wasn't too worried about the anger because I'd twice seen my ability to manhandle Amos when provoked.

"I love her," he continued, "but I knew we were too different to be a man and wife." He blushed, noticeable even in the dim light. "But I had not yet thought of her with another man."

"Ah," I said, nodding, "so Katie's been leaving her boots under another cowboy's bed."

Amos stopped midstride and flashed a glare my way. "She is pure," he said. There were elements of a snarl in his tone. "Do not ever insult her with such comments about her boots."

I shrugged. "Sorry. If she hasn't been unfaithful, what's the issue with another man?"

"His name is John Yoder, and I despise him." The pacing resumed. "We have never liked each other, and as we became older, we were good at not being in the same place. But now ..."

"Why can't you stand him?" I asked.

"Because!" Amos threw his arms up in one wild, frustrated gesture. "John Yoder is prideful, and he likes too much the women who are pretty. When we were in school together, he would spend all his time getting others to laugh but would blame me for the loud noises from students." He paused, and I, for one, hoped there'd be more dirt than liking pretty girls and getting one's name on the board. "John Yoder is the Slim Shady."

I winced. There are perils to picking up slang without any outside monitoring. "And John and Katie are dating?"

Amos rolled his eyes. "The Amish do not do dating. They get married."

"They get married without dating first?" From where I stood, dateless for a good five years, I could see the perks.

"Let me explain to you...." He massaged his face, and I could hear the quiet percussion of a day's beard. "Girls and boys spend time together but with other girls and boys. Then a boy drives a girl to her house in his buggy. And if he likes her, and she likes him, they lie in bed together all night talking."

I snickered. It was very seventh-grade of me to do so, but really? All night in bed, talking? Did he think I was completely stupid? I asked him as much.

"Yes, of course they talk. What else would they do in the middle of the night?" He wrinkled his brow in honest confusion. Then the light dawned. "Oh, I know what you think." He shook his head. Disappointment attached itself to his frown. "The English do not know how to talk all night in bed. The English like to—what was that word—it rhymes with nag? Snag?"

"All right, all right." I stopped him. "That will do. I will have you know," I said, posture as indignant as I could manage on a playground swing, "not all Englishers are unable to control themselves. In bed or otherwise."

"Well, that might be the truth," he said. "But Amish girls and boys wait until they are married. First, we lie in bed and talk. Plus," he added, jabbing the air for emphasis, "at least my community let us use the beds. Some Amish make the boy sit up in a rocking chair all night with the girl on his lap." He shuddered. "Very awkward."

I stared at him. He *looked* like a regular guy, other than the shirt, but he *sounded* like an alien.

"So this is your employment." He clapped his hands together. "You must go back to my home and take secret information to show me if Katie lies in bed with John."

This from the man who didn't like my boots metaphor. "You want actual photos of the two in bed? I mean, I can do that. Done it plenty of times, in fact—"

"No, no, please." Amos looked sick. "I want you to listen secretly and tell me what you hear. It will be easy." He shrugged. "You need only to watch them together one time to see if they are to be married. Katie will show it on her face. She always did with me."

The boy scuffed the toe of his shoe into the dirt and slumped the slump of the dumped. If I were a romantic, which I'm not, it probably would have made me burst into tears and order up some ice cream for purposes of emotional eating.

"Will you work as my Magnum PI?" he said. His big blue eyes were all mopey, and even though I didn't know a thing about rocking-chair dating or buggy cruises, I said I would.

"Let me do some research," I said. "When I have a good handle on your people, the geography of the area, my surveillance MO, I'll contact you for our next meeting."

He nodded. "Geography."

"See you at the golf course," I said. I rose from the swing, hating for that small second that I didn't have a real office with thick blinds and a lazy ceiling fan. I put out my hand. "Get some sleep. You'll need to have all your faculties for the road ahead." I didn't mean to make my voice all gravelly, but when it did, I kind of liked it.

"I will sleep," Amos said, making his voice scratchy too, which completely ruined it for me.

"Later." I waved and trotted to the edge of the playground. I didn't look back but pictured Amos staring after me, watching my impressive athleticism-in-training, readying myself for the opposition. I imagined his view of me becoming blurry with distance, the fog cutting jagged fingers through the night. "The truth cannot hide," I huffed in my gravelly voice, my eyes practicing their slits while my feet carried me home.

7

Bring in the Experts

Nothing like finding one's purpose in life to make all the other stuff bearable. In the days following my first debriefing for Operation Bonnet, I approached all the lackluster elements of my life with new gusto. When the cleaning service ditched out on us and left the on-course restrooms filthy, I agreed to do it without making Tank suffer.

"Tank," I said, putting a hand on his shoulder, "I'm happy to lend a hand, though I'll be sure to cover it with a rubber glove, heh heh!"

He watched me leave the clubhouse, and I must admit, Pollyanna toting a toilet brush was a new character even to me. If I swiveled my head about forty-five degrees to the south, I'd see the root of my transformation: Amos the Amish boy working on the miniature-golf course, representing all of my newfound freedom, my first tough case, and the doorway to the career I was born to dominate. I pulled on the yellow gloves and whistled on my way to the twelfth hole.

Friday afternoon, I cut out of work early with the excuse of a doctor's appointment. I raised my eyebrows when I told Tank, knowing that the mere suggestion of a female going to her doctor would conjure up enough scariness that I'd need say no more.

"Yes, of course, yes, the doctor. An APPOINTMENT. Hope everything works out ALL RIGHT." He reached out to slap me on the head, but I stopped him with an outstretched hand.

"Tank." I shook my head. "Please. It's a fragile time."

"Right, absolutely." Poor guy looked pained.

"Well," I said, sobriety filling my voice, "I'll let you know how everything turns out."

"Oh, that's not really necessary," he said, backing into a display and rushing to stop a freefall of T-shirts. "I'll just see you tomorrow. Call in SICK if you need to."

I thought I heard him say the call-in-sick part, but his face was very close to the T-shirts at that moment and I didn't have the heart to ask him to repeat himself. If I'd ever considered having children, which I hadn't, I would feel very pleased that women were the ones appointed for that task. The men in my circle couldn't spit out the word *obstetrician* without brandishing the nearest cotton crew neck XL in self-defense.

I grabbed my bag and new spiral-bound notebook and let myself out the employees-only exit. My BMW SUV, black with camel interior, sat just a ways off from the other beaters in the employee lot. I started 'er up and felt a small surge of happiness as the leather quickly cooled under my rear.

Living as the sole heir to a substantial fortune had perks, more than I deemed to accept most days. Room and board at the Monroe estate were free, of course, though I put in my time taking care of Nona, cooking most of our meals, and keeping tabs on the house. Mother and

Pop were paying for my college tuition, but I insisted on using my paychecks from Tank for any other living expenses. My phone, my clothes, my entertainment, my new Elite—these were Nellie purchases, every one. This was a somewhat unpopular decision in our house, but I held my ground. I figured in forty years or so, when I'd solved the nation's most complicated criminal cases and had made a mint from brilliance, toil, and speaking engagements, I could spoil myself and employ the occasional cabana boy. But from the start, I wanted to be in charge of my income, beholden to no one in my gene pool.

Except for the car. Oh, the car. I turned up my nose when Pop first mentioned it as a beginning-college gift. I was perfectly content, I'd reminded him, driving my humble but reliable 1999 Honda Civic. But what the Germans can do to a car … well. I was simply no match for it once Pop brought it home for a test run. I wouldn't have pegged myself as one to nurse a vehicular weakness, but there it was, tooling along nicely on Maywood Boulevard, delivering me to the front doors of Claremont College like I was Jackie O. stepping out of Bergdorf's. Only the hair separated us.

When I passed through the double doors, the two-story lobby greeted me with all the coldness it had the first day of classes four semesters before. The dominant color scheme in the whole of Claremont relied heavily on gray. Many incarnations—a surprising variety, really—but all gray. I followed the linoleum around the corner, took a quick left, and walked to the end of the hall. When I reached the final door on the right, I rapped a knuckle right by the name placard: *Dr. Sonya Moss, Professor of Religious Studies.*

She threw open the door, one hand smoothing a barrette halfheartedly positioned in her hair above her right ear.

"Nellie! Why, it's you!" She smiled, and I could see she'd had either spinach or basil since the last time she'd brushed.

I crooked my index finger and poked it into my own teeth.

"Oop, oh," she said, scurrying back to her desk and letting the heavy door fall onto my shoulder. "I had a, um"—she riffled through the top drawer of her desk and emerged with a toothpick—"pad Thai for lunch? Sweet little place down on Cedar?" She took a moment to extract the green things before continuing. "Thanks for letting me know. Fresh basil, fragrant but also tenacious." She laughed and revealed that her work in her mouth was not done. I had no more stomach for it, though, so I launched into the reason for my visit.

"Professor Moss, I'm looking for information, and I know you're the one to help me."

She gestured for me to sit. I hefted a pile of books off the chair and set it down amid the stacks that lined each wall. Metal bookshelves loomed around and above me, burgeoning with titles like *Buddha and Jesus: A Definitive Comparison through a Postmodern Lens* and *Hinduism under the Gupta Empire*. It was not difficult to imagine sleeping in that room.

"I'm happy to help, Nellie. You were an exceptional student in Intro to Religious Studies.… You know," she said, lowering her voice, "you would be an excellent major." Her eyebrows reached up her pale forehead to her hairline.

"No, I really wouldn't," I said. "To tell you the truth, I'd be bored out of my gourd."

Professor Moss looked slightly unnerved, and I realized that she might take offense that not everyone loved reading sermons by very,

very dead men. Perhaps there was more to it than that, but I was there to talk about Amos.

"I need to know about the Amish."

"Ooohh," she said, leaning forward in her chair as if energized by the thought. "The Amish. You know that's why I live here, right? To be closer to them?"

I did know that, as she'd mentioned it in pretty much every lecture during REL 101. Professor Moss had the uncanny ability to work the Amish into every religious group we'd studied. Buddhism, for example, reminded her of the Amish with its emphasis on simplicity and prayer. Jewish men wore yarmulkes, just like the Amish with their hats and bonnets. Even that wily Martin Luther reminded her of the Amish with his love for a good hymn-sing. I mean, honestly. I *knew* I was in the right place.

"In fact, I had offers from Wellesley and William and Mary, but I had to accept Claremont's position because then I could be only *forty miles* from the nearest Amish settlement. Forty miles! That's a hop and a skip!" Her cheeks flushed to a touch of pink. I wanted her to eat more red meat. "How can I help you, Nellie? Are you researching a paper? Taking an American history course this summer?"

"Right. Something like that." I let my eyes wander a bit around the room. "You could call it an independent study."

"Ah," she said, nodding. "The best learning occurs out of one's own interests. I remember—" she said, pausing to giggle, "—I remember when my mom and dad sat me down in junior high and asked me to stop reading all those Amish romances. And they wanted me to stop practicing my German. They were worried that I was becoming too singularly focused at such a young age." She shook her head. "I had to wear a bonnet only in my room, they said. The neighbors were talking, they said. But look at me now!"

I joined her in looking around the room she'd indicated with a flourish of her hand. A near-dead fern sat in the corner. Two paintings of Amish-looking women sat propped on top of one bookshelf. Draped over a Kleenex box was a knitted brown-and-orange crocheted number. In summary, I was depressed.

"Well, congratulations on a dream fulfilled," I said. "Can you get me in?"

"I'm sorry, 'in' to what?" She stopped. "The Amish?"

"Yes. I need access to the group outside Springville."

"Oh, heavenly days, no."

Have you ever heard sea lions at the zoo? She laughed a bit like they bark. It was a startling moment.

"No," she said after the barking subsided. "They don't look favorably on English visitors. I myself have only recently started to earn the trust of one family, and that's after three years of cautious persistence."

"I'm fairly persistent," I said. "And I wouldn't make fun of them or try to hijack any buggies."

Professor Moss looked confused. "I'm afraid, Nellie, the only way I can help you learn about the Amish is through written sources." She swiveled in her chair to the bookcase behind her desk. "This," she said, letting a tome drop onto the papers in front of me, "is the definitive work on Amish history in America. I would start with that."

I paged through the book, ready to fight fire with fire. "Ah, yes, Kraybill," I said. "I've come across him many times in my preliminary research. What do you think of his take on the schism with Menno Simons?" *Let us give thanks in one accord for the glories of Internet research.*

The fire worked. Moss looked like she might cry or dance, neither of which I wanted to witness, but both had the potential of helping a girl out. "Oh, you've hit on the classic discussion, Nellie. Very bright of you indeed. Illuminating, in fact."

If she only knew.

"I have witnessed the effects of this schism many times, even in the Schrock family. The matriarch, Grandmother Mary, has been the most talkative with me, and she has often mentioned the moral concerns she has for the Mennonite church."

"Understandable. Look at what they've allowed in: the car driving, the zippers, the pursuit of higher education. Pretty much morality slackers."

"Well, of course, *I* have no issue with those activities, but the Amish do, particularly the Old Order to which our Springville neighbors belong."

"This Granny Mary, does she just sit down and talk with you over coffee?"

"It's *Grandmother* Mary, and she rarely sits down, to tell you the truth." Professor Moss began rummaging around in a drawer. "She talks with me while she bakes. I've been compiling a database of Old Order Amish recipes, which is the only way I've found to get a woman within the community to speak frankly." She shrugged. "I'm not a cook and don't care to be, but if I have to roll out pastry dough for three hours to get a woman to talk with me about what it's like to be Amish and female in the twenty-first century, doggone it, I will."

Pastry, I thought with a small smile. *The great equalizer.*

"Here she is," Professor Moss said. She held up a photo for me to see. "Grandmother Mary."

I looked long and hard before speaking. "Her back, you mean."

"Well, yes, of course." Professor Moss snatched the photo back and took another look herself. "She'd never let me take a photo of her face. This one was snapped as she was walking to the barn for eggs." She winked at me, and I felt pity surge through me. The woman had a long way to go before tooting her own stealth horn.

I gathered the reference book into my arms and stood. "I'll start by reading this." I thumped it once with my index finger, and the professor winced. "And," I added, "I'll take good care of it. Thank you."

"Not at all," she said, recovered from the book abuse. "I'm happy to help. You keep me posted on what you discover in those pages, Nellie. It just might change your academic life forever, as it did mine."

I waved and returned a cheery smile, already feeling my mouth water for a healthy slice of strudel.

8

Rules of the Game

I handed Amos a third napkin. He tucked it under the malt but continued slurping. When he plunked the empty glass onto the table, the chocolate had formed a foamy 'stache on his upper lip.

"The chocolate malts are super-duper." Against my advice, Amos had been watching a marathon of *Gidget* reruns. "I can't refrain from eating too much of them. Do you always love the very, very cold things?"

"Um, sure. Not like dry ice or anything that drastic, but I can appreciate a Coke on the rocks."

"The Coke is also better frozen. And you can put inside the Coke glass a chunk of ice cream. Not homemade ice cream but ice cream that comes on big trucks and has been frozen for weeks, maybe months."

An interesting take on food preservatives. I'd never realized their romance.

"Right. Well, you go ahead and tackle your second malt," I said, watching Amos tug on the next frosted glass in the lineup. If *he* wasn't able to keep from mixing business with pleasure, I'd have to tow that rope alone. "I wanted to update you on my progress with Operation Bonnet."

Amos scrunched his nose over the glass and a poof of cool air rose from the ice cream. "This is a dumb name."

I bristled. "No, it's not. It's clever." It was.

"This is not groovy, using bonnet in the name. It is too obvious to other people. What about …?" He paused to take a slow sip in his straw. "What about Operation Moondoggie?"

I stared. "Please tell me you are joking and would like to apologize for calling my idea dumb."

He shook his head. "This is the serious, best name. Moondoggie is Gidget's name for her boyfriend. A secret code name. It is a perfect relationship: Gidget is to Moondoggie as I am to Katie." His expression was grave, even as he said the word *moondoggie* twice in one monologue.

I sighed. Who was I to crush the romantic hopes of one wayfaring Amish malt drinker? "Fine. But we'll call it Operation M for short."

"Fine." He looked pleased. "This is a choice you will not be regretting. So," he said, sitting up at attention, "what is the news you have for me?"

I pushed away my plate, recently emptied of a Reuben and fries. Frank's Diner on the east side made the best of both, and it was my pleasure to partake, even if I had to witness malt inhalation.

"Let's cut to it," I said. I leaned over the table slightly and wanted with every fiber of my being to use my gravelly voice, but the room vibrated with conversation, banging flatware, and calls from the kitchen. I settled for eye slits. "I'm going in. I'm going to meet Katie."

"Oh, this is very fast moving." Amos swallowed hard. He cracked each knuckle on his right hand, one by one, so slowly I wanted to reach over and finish it for him. "Are you certain this plan is effective?"

"Absolutely," I said, bravado inching its way into my voice. "I have a contact and will be using the connection I make with her to gather info on Katie and John."

Amos's eyes widened. "Who is this contact?"

I lowered my voice, as if some unsuspecting Amish person was hiding under our booth. "Mary Schrock."

Amos froze and then burst into laughter. "Grandmother Mary? She—she—" he started but then broke off again in what can only be described as an undignified man-giggle.

I waited, watching as he doubled over onto the table, nose inches from the sparkly Formica. "When you get control of yourself, I'd love to hear why you're laughing." I used one of Amos's napkins to brush crumbs into a little pile. "While we wait, I'd like to remind you I'm here to *help*, but since you seem to think my ideas are inferior...."

"I will apologize," he said, taking a deep breath. Aggressively mocking a person takes it out of you. "You are not inferior. It is only that Mary Schrock"—and he nearly started back in with the laughing—"well, you will see her. She will show you an interesting representing of the Amish." He let out one last chortle, and I found him convincingly unattractive.

I sniffed. "She's a grandma, and she belongs to a religious group that values hard work, simplicity, and keeping to itself. How interesting can she be?"

Amos smiled and seemed to look through me as he spoke. "I will want to hear of your time with her. The Amish are not all like the pretty pictures on calendars. Or that movie *Witness* with Indiana Jones."

"Well, of course I know that." I rolled my eyes because I was feeling just that insulted. "I'd say any nostalgic notion about that movie fully evaporated when we found out Kelly McGillis bats for the other team."

Amos gasped, and I nodded in sympathy. It had come as a shock for so many *Top Gun* fans.

"Do you mean," he said, motionless across from me, "that she is now a baseball player? Can a woman do that?"

"I mean …" I said slowly, then retreated. No need to be the one to drop the bomb. He'd have enough *Access Hollywood* moments ahead of him now that he was English. "I mean that movies are never honest representations of the truth. I'm assuming Granny looks and acts nothing like Kelly. Or Harrison." I turned to a fresh page in my notebook and poised a pen above the blank space. "Anything else I need to know before heading back to your old stomping grounds?"

"Hmm." He dipped a french fry into the malt glass. "Many things you will understand when you are there. For now, you should remember not to wear any clothes that look like you are a prostitute."

I raised an eyebrow and waited.

He indicated with a nod toward the notebook that I should be writing this down.

I cleared my throat. "Amos, you'll find that women in the English world don't really like being compared to prostitutes. For their clothes or for any other reason."

Color spread on his cheeks. "I am sorry. I do not mean you are a prostitute. You are a Magnum PI, and you can hit men with much force in your fists. I only mean to say that you cannot wear things that show your body or the shape of your body. This is for husbands only to see."

"Right," I said, making a note. "Bod for hubby alone."

He continued. "And you should not wear this." He pointed to my lips. "No shiny liquids."

"Lip gloss?" My mother would be so saddened. It had taken her years to get me to wear the stuff, and now that I was finally starting to tolerate it, I had a great reason to leave all shiny liquids at home. "Got it. What else?"

"You should not try to physically injure other people." He stared at me with solemn eyes.

"Amos," I said, trying to be patient, "I only attacked out of self-defense."

He shrugged. "If you punch people, they will not let you come back. The Amish are pacifists."

I sighed. "Any other pearls of wisdom?"

He thought for a moment. "Do not take photos. This will also get you expelled. No cussing words, no musical instruments, no electric appliances."

I wrote for a moment. "So I'll leave home my f-bombs, my clarinet, and my blender." I shut the notebook and stood, dropping a twenty on the table to pay for our lunch. "If you think of anything else, call me before Tuesday afternoon. That's when I go to the Schrock farm for the first time."

He looked past me, face drawn in thought. "You might see one of my sisters or Katie walking along the road by the Schrock house. There is an orchard beside there where we used to go."

I watched his face. His eyes shone with memories, a bit like Nona's during a good story. I put my hand on his shoulder as I passed. He sighed deeply, and I knew I could leave without saying good-bye.

I got back to the golf course as Tank was hammering a sign onto a tree by the cart corral.

"Hey, Tank," I said as I came up behind him. I read over his shoulder, "*No Chewing Tobacco Allowed On CARTS or COURSE!* Wow," I said. "Did you have that custom-made?"

"You'd better BELIEVE it." He squatted down and retrieved his box of nails. "You'd think I wouldn't have to MAKE a sign, but I'm not cleaning out any more TABACKY from my cup holders!" He hooked his thumb through a belt loop and took in his handiwork. "Born in BARNS, some people. And it makes a man sick and TIRED."

"I don't blame you," I said. We began walking toward the clubhouse. "Listen, before I forget, I saw Amos at lunch, and he wanted me to thank you again for giving him the afternoon off. Said it was the nicest thing any employer's ever done for him."

Tank shook his head. He held the door for me, and I headed to the front counter. "You know what I think?" Tank's voice dropped to a scratchy whisper.

I waited.

"I think those Amish kids have a heckuva time growing up. I think that Amos has worked himself near to DEATH and that's why he escaped." Tank was never one to deny himself the pleasure of dramatic narrative. The man *tsk*ed. "And I've heard they don't BELIEVE in birthday parties! Not even for children!"

"Um, maybe you're confusing the Amish with Jehovah's Witnesses. They're the ones who aren't into holidays."

"What?" Tank looked dismayed. "Michael JACKSON was a Jehovah's Witness. Nobody ever gave him a BIRTHDAY party?" He shook his head and rubbed his close-cropped gray hair. "No wonder that kid was MESSED UP."

The bell over the front screen door trembled, announcing the arrival of a family of five. Dad and the oldest, a gangly girl of about eight years, headed straight for the vending machines. The mother, who looked like she hadn't slept very well for seven years, herded twin boys of around kindergarten age toward me.

"Excuse me, miss, do you have a public restroom?"

Both of the kids were hopping in place.

"In the back, first door on your right."

She trotted after the boys as they sped toward the back, knocking over a half-mannequin and a golf bag on their way. I cringed to think of the animal-like markings I was sure to find around the toilet seat when I went to clean it that afternoon.

"Thanks now," the mom said when they returned an impressive two minutes later. She adjusted her visor and issued a slew of uninterrupted commands aiming to gather her brood into the waiting cart. Not one of the children appeared to be listening to her words, but somehow, they all circled first the store and then the cart enough times that momentary weariness propelled them into a more submissive state, and they were off to play eighteen. I watched them drive in a crooked trajectory toward the first hole and felt myself counting down to Tuesday and the first day of my real life.

Two hours later, a wall of dark clouds began a stately procession across the western sky. Tank and I stood by his *tabacky* sign, musing about when the storm would hit full force, when the family of five came careening over the hill by the ninth green. I could hear at least two children wailing. The dad was in the driver's seat and taking a corner at a speed not appropriate in an electric vehicle. The mother had one hand over her eyes, head tipped slightly forward, the other hand gripping the side of the cart with such strength, I could see the whites of her knuckles from forty yards away.

"I *know*, Dan," she was saying as they neared the clubhouse. "But there's such a thing as *quality time.*"

Dan braked so hard the tires skidded. He looked up at Tank's disapproving stare and mumbled an apology. "Josie, Jordy, Johnny, in the car." The kids, two of them sniffling, tumbled out of the cart and dragged their feet on the pavement as they walked to a teal minivan.

"Thanks a lot," Mom said to Tank. She followed her husband and called over her shoulder, "Lovely course. We'll be back!"

The husband muttered something under his breath, and Tank whistled. "Rough round. Those two SHORT ones might be too young to appreciate the game."

I nodded. "Some of us never get to that level of appreciation."

Tank turned to me. "Nellie Augusta Lourdes Monroe, it is nothing but a TRAGEDY that the daughter of Clive Monroe doesn't care for the game of golf. And the worst part?" He pointed one cigar-like finger at me. "The worst part is that I've SEEN your swing, and it's a DEAD RINGER for your father's! A little fine tuning and YOU'D be a STAR!"

I could see the words pained him, visions of clean putting and birdie-worthy chipping out of the rough prancing around his head. "Sorry, Tank," I said. "I identify more with the wailing twin boys than with you and Pop. You've tried your best to convince me otherwise, and if you couldn't do it, Payne Stewart himself would fall short."

"Oh, now don't bring up Payne." He bit his lower lip, and I knew if we took that conversation down the road often traveled, he'd be in tears within minutes.

"How about this?" I clapped my hands to distract him. It sounds a bit like a preschool teacher, I know, but believe me, no one wants to see Tank cry. A *lot* of sinus fluid is involved. "How about we head back in the clubhouse and start inventory while we wait out the storm?" I held the door for him.

"Go home," he said. "I'll finish up here and lock up early. NO one will be heading out to play in this weather."

"You sure?" I asked. I watched his face to make sure the Payne story wasn't still looming in his thoughts. Tank looked all the part of a brute, but he was the biggest, gray-domed teddy bear on the planet. I didn't want to leave him feeling down.

"I'm POSITIVE, young lady." He smiled a goofy grin. "I do NOT want to see that head of hair after a rain storm." He shuddered for effect, but it looked more like a shimmy.

"Nice moves," I said. I punched my time card and turned when Tank said nothing. He was waiting for me to see him dancing a mix of the Cabbage Patch and the Sprinkler next to the front counter. Don't visualize it.

"Bye, Tank." I shook my head but couldn't contain a laugh.

"I'm KNOWN for my moves," he sang as he Cabbage Patched me right out the door.

9

Table Talk

I stopped going to the talented-and-gifted classes about the same time I started cooking. Once I figured out how much time teachers wasted during the school day, I gave up homework entirely. Instead, I filled the hours between school and bed with reading everything Robert Ludlum wrote, going on walks with Nona, or talking on the teen line with Matt. With the advantage of maturity, I now see I was extremely bored and in need of a challenge. At the time, though, I just thought I was hungry.

Annette might not have known how to toss her own salad, but she did subscribe to highbrow periodicals, most notably *Fine Cooking*, *Gourmet*, and *Bon Appétit.* I began paging through them after school, holding them in human hands after they'd spent years in artfully arranged neglect on the coffee table. It was during one of the teen-line conversations that I first discovered the world outside catered meals.

"Mmm," I said into my hot-pink phone, cord twisting around my fingers, "goat cheese tarts with heirloom-tomato salad."

"I'm pretty sure you shouldn't make a tart with anything goat related," Matt said.

"Smoked chicken with wheat berries and bacon."

"Skip the wheat, triple the bacon."

"Oh. Wow. Lamb chops with fresh herbs and roasted figs."

"What's a fig? Sounds garden of Eden-ish."

Matt was not a great help in those years, but once I got some practice in and started asking him over for dinner, he stopped making fun of goat cheese, though he never gave up an undying ardor for bacon. This is the thought that propelled me under the tumultuous sky to TasteWay as I drove home from work. I sprinted through the parking lot to the sliding-glass doors. The rain had not begun in earnest, but the clouds were impatient and had begun leaking heavy drops onto the warm earth.

"Well, lookie-loo who's here!"

I heard Misty Warren-Pitz before I had finished wiping the rain out of my eyes. "Nellie Monroe, town genius!" She was smiling, but I could hear the bite undergirding the compliment. Misty was not one to mess with when in an irritable state, not when we were prepubescent and not since we'd grown to real people.

"Hi, Misty, gotta-run-see-you-later." I made my greeting one long word with hopes that she'd take the hint and back off the town genius. It must have worked because I looked behind me as I was gathering spring carrots and mushrooms and was relieved to find I was alone in produce. I walked through the aisles, gathering what I needed for dinner, and only ran into Misty on the way out of the store. She stood between the sets of double doors, eyes and frown focused on the downpour. She glanced at me as I pulled the hood of my sweatshirt over my head and tucked in bundles of afro around my neck.

"You could just *cut* the thing and be done with it," she snarled.

It was disheartening to know a woman who snarled.

"Thanks for the input," I said, forcing my tone upward even as I felt my stomach sink. Sometimes you can't take the thirteen-year-old out of a girl, genius or not.

"No problem," she said quietly.

I stood in front of the sensor and waited as the doors parted. The wind was picking up, and it nudged a spray of raindrops into the lobby entry.

"Hey," Misty said as I started to walk, "I'm pregnant."

I turned. Her eyes were big and fearful.

"Congratulations," I said but felt immediately unsure it was the right sentiment.

"Just thought I'd tell you. Before everyone in town is talking about it over their beer." She laughed sharply and then turned to face the rain.

"Thanks." I waited a beat and then shrugged deeper within my sweatshirt. I ran into the storm, wondering how I'd been elected genius, target, and priest all in the same encounter.

Thunder split the sky with a hungry rumble as I dropped the pasta into boiling water.

"Is that Nadine's?" Nona munched on a sliver of white cheddar as she watched me.

"It is," I said, pleased that she noticed. Nadine was Casper's resident Italian lady. She'd run her own restaurant for years and had handed it over to her children a decade ago. When she got the time or the inclination, she still made small batches of fresh pasta and sold them to TasteWay. If you were there at the right time, you could take home a pound of handmade ravioli, melt-in-your-mouth gnocchi, or as I had, ribbons of pappardelle that cried out for fresh vegetables and a white wine sauce.

"Hi, ladies." The back door to the kitchen swung shut behind Matt. "You're both looking lovely this evening."

Nona turned her cheek for a kiss, and Matt leaned down to oblige.

Sometimes when I saw Matt, I'd think of my childhood blanket, Pookie. I never tried to sniff him or rub his satin trimming or anything, but the feeling was the same. So familiar, so comfortable, I could close my eyes and see the imprint of the details without a look: thick hair the color of pecan pie, slightly disheveled and caramel-touched during the summer. Glasses that had morphed with five-year increments, the most notable being "the goggs" of late elementary, which were only slightly smaller than aviator goggles and a zippy shade of green. Wide hazel eyes that focused a democratic curiosity on everything from zoo animals to effervescent Junior League members. Long and lanky after a growth spurt the summer of our freshman year of high school, when he grew four inches in three months but the needle stayed put on the scale.

I cleared my throat, knowing without a glance that he had mischief on his face. "Flattery and kisses. I'm afraid the effect is inauthenticity."

He pulled out the stool next to Nona. "What about flattery and kisses isn't authentic? I'm nothing if not sincere." He slouched into the seat and let one edge of his mouth tinker with a smile.

I rolled my eyes, but Nona patted his hand. "Of course you're being sincere, Matthew." He allowed precisely one person to call him that, and Nona was she. "You are the sweetest boy in town, and Nellie knows it." She dropped her voice to a stage whisper. "She's just feeling prickly tonight. Something about work."

Matt raised his eyebrows, which for him was the equivalent of shock and dismay. "What happened? Did she finally quit and decide to devote herself to curing cancer, just like we all know she can?"

Nona giggled. "Now that you say it—"

I sighed. "I'm in the room. Can anyone hear me speaking? Because I could just do that and save you some trouble."

"Oh! Nellie! How are you?" Matt's eyes twinkled. "You're looking lovely this evening."

I took a sharp knife to the bacon. "I'm adding this to your pasta, bratface. Everyone else would be happy with vegetables, but I knew you'd want some sort of pork product as a garnish."

"Now, don't be so tough on him." Nona again with the hand patting. "If you're honest with yourself, Nellie, you'll agree it will taste better with bacon."

It's a low moment when one's grandmother takes sides with meat over her own granddaughter.

"Thanks for the pork product," Matt said. He pulled the plate of cheddar and almonds closer and picked up a wedge of cheese. "What happened at work?"

I tossed the veggies in the sauté pan one last time and turned off the heat. "It wasn't really at work, per se." I drew the words out, concentrating on draining the pasta into a colander. Squinting my eyes into the steam bath, I said, "Misty Warren-Pitz is pregsy."

Nona clapped once and cooed. "Oh, a baby. We need more babies in this town."

Matt looked confused. "Um," he said, pointing a cheese slice at Nona, "first, I don't really understand what that means. Second," he said, pointing at me, "Misty Pitz knocked up makes you prickly? Isn't it kind of funny to think of her all front heavy? And wearing a beret?" Spit escaped with his guffaw.

"Gross. No spitting on the food." I carried two plates over to the eat-in booth by the windows. The waning daylight shimmered in pockets of yellow warmth, making every green of the garden vie for our approval. The original Byrnes built the dining room to impress, but they added the kitchen booth fifty years into the house's life as a concession for small children. I'd long since stopped needing Mrs. H. to cut my meat but still preferred a meal by the window over a stuffy feast in the dining room any day of my week.

"I love this spot," Nona said. She scooted into the booth, close to the window, her eyes following the movement of dappled light on the grass. "Remember the time I sat down for dinner in the dining room and the Johnsons were there? Oh, they were a prudish lot. Not a good night to do the splits." She giggled.

I waited, silencing Matt with a quick shake of my head. This was going to be a doozy of a story, and I didn't want Nona to get distracted.

"Margot Johnson had an ironclad lack of warmth. She used to wrinkle her nose whenever anyone said anything remotely romantic. I'll bet she wore three pairs of underwear, just in case her husband tried anything marital. Poor Ted," she said, shaking her head. A hummingbird flew right up close to the window and made Nona smile. She took a deep breath and turned to me. "Nellie, you're such a good girl to cook dinner tonight. What did you make?"

I pushed her plate gently toward her. "Pasta by Nadine, Nona. I hope you like it." I bit the inside of my cheek and could feel Matt's eyes on me. *Everything's fine*, I said with my posture, with the way I attacked my first bite of pasta. *Don't be nice to me right now because I might lose it.*

"So," I said too loudly, "I have great news. I have my first job as a PI."

Nona put down her fork and gathered me in a side hug. "That's just wonderful," she said. "I knew success was just around the bend."

I felt her weathered hands grip me around the shoulders, and I leaned into her.

"Sweet," Matt said. He brushed a passel of stray crumbs into an open hand before continuing. For being a man without a discernible pulse, Matt was nothing but fastidious when it came to table manners. "What's the story?"

I shook my head. "Can't say."

"What?" Matt frowned. "I'm your best friend." He turned to Nona and added, "And best-looking, but who's keeping score?"

She giggled.

"After the countless conversations we've had that have revolved around your PI dreams, you owe me, Monroe. Give it up."

I twirled noodles around my fork and said nothing.

"Oh, you've got to be kidding." Matt's voice took on an uncharacteristic urgency, and I smiled to hear him almost emote. "At least tell me who hired you. Do I know him? Her?"

I shrugged. "More bread, Nona?" I asked.

She took a slice. "Thank you, dear. The pasta is delicious. Matthew, have you tried yours? You seem awfully worked up about something. Eat a bit and take a breather."

Matt stared at me, and I smiled. "Obey your elder, Matthew. Partake."

He shook his head. "After all these years …"

"Listen," I said, softening, "I'm not trying to hold out on you. Professional ethics require discretion, that's all. I work for my client, and his or her best wishes are my ultimate concern." *His or her.* Wasn't that perfect?

We ate in silence, the only sounds ones of utility: a fork hitting the plate, the crank of the pepper mill, the optimistic music of ice cubes on glass.

Matt finally cleared his throat. "Fine," he said. He tore a piece of bread off a new slice. "Just don't come crying to me when you need help cracking the case. Or getting a good deal on technology," he added. "We'll just keep our professional lives to ourselves."

"Sounds fair," I said and offered the peace pipe. "I made double-chocolate cherry brownies this morning. That is, if you're not too worked up to eat."

"Nellie, you're shameless," Nona said. She winked at me. "Hit me with a big one, please. À la mode."

"Matt?" I rose from the table.

He nodded. "Yes, please," he mumbled.

"Cream and sugar with your coffee?"

He grinned but met my eyes only briefly. "It's really good you're a great cook. It makes me consider forgiveness as a viable option."

"Excellent," I said and went to cut generous squares of repentance.

10

Orientation

I walked up the long dirt driveway, noting pronounced ruts marking the paths of buggy wheels, and felt nerves churn flips in my belly. *Maybe this is how soldiers feel on the eve of battle,* I mused. Or runners during the quiet moments before the gun fires to start the race. Or poser detectives who have only online certificates to prove their competence.

"You'll be fine," I said aloud, scuffing one black boot in the dirt. "You look the part, you'll act the part, you're made for this work, so prove it. Prove it. Prove it. Prove it." The words became a cheer, then a sort of creepy incantation. I cleared my throat. Here it was finally game time, and I was doubting my destiny. It's a little known fact, but even brilliant people doubt themselves. You know how Lincoln failed getting elected multiple times before he became president and how Einstein was dyslexic and socially distrusted because of his hair? I'm just saying, it happens to the best of us, and I tried to remember that as I approached the Schrocks' white farmhouse.

My legs were already feeling itchy and hot underneath the skirt. Amos had wondered about my decision to wear the Amish costume, but I'd stood firm. When in Rome, I'd assured him. Plus, the idea was for me to *blend in,* to become *one* with his people so that the women would forget I was an outsider and trust me implicitly and tell me anything I wanted to know. This kind of relationship needed care, starting with my ensemble. The Schrocks weren't about to deposit their secrets with a girl in a tube top, I told him. I didn't technically own a tube top, but it was a powerful image, one that clearly got through to Amos.

"All right," he'd said at last. "I understand your forceful opinion. I will pray that this idea works." Then as an afterthought, "At least you will not be like Roxanne, you do not need to wear that dress tonight." He started to hum in falsetto.

"Thanks for the input," I said over the music. "I'll call you when I get home."

"Yes, OK." He made a hang-loose sign with his thumb and pinky. "Toodles."

How was he even watching *Gidget?* The Hallmark Channel? A box set?

I'd found a pair of black stockings in my mother's closet. They were actually a leopard print, but I didn't think anyone would have their noses close enough to notice. From what I'd read thus far about the Amish, they were not big on noses near legs. Plus the long skirt would dissuade even the most curious. Courtesy of my neighborhood Goodwill, the skirt was sky blue cotton. It had a ton of pleats and poofed out a bit around the waist and rear. Not my best silhouette, but I would take one for the modesty team if it meant good intel. I topped my look with a plain dark blue button-down and was nearly good to go. But I'd needed a bonnet, and Amos was no help.

He'd looked at me like I was a few cards short. "I do not own any bonnet. I am a man."

"I *know* that," I'd said. Honestly. "But where can I get one?"

"Of course you must sew one." He said this like he was describing how to open one's gas cap on one's car, stupid woman driver.

"I don't sew."

He shrugged. "I do not sew either. Perhaps you can ask a woman who does not attack people?"

I would never live that down.

As I could not sew and knew no one in town who would accommodate such a request without an inquisition, I'd turned to Johnny Cavell's Dance and Costume Magic, a Casper curiosity since 1968. Johnny was roughly seven thousand years old by my count. He'd smoked since he was five, and his voice barely registered on human ear frequencies. As a child, I'd thought Johnny was living but gnarled proof that we were not alone in the universe. As an adult, I was still open to the possibilities of his true origins.

One great thing about Johnny, though, was that he didn't give a high-hootin' holler what you were going to do with a bonnet. The one I procured was very much Ma Ingalls and not as much Girl Amish. It was large, so large that I couldn't exactly employ any peripheral vision as I walked up to the house. To see clearly on either side I had to rotate my entire upper body. In other circumstances, such as if I were a part of the chorus in *Oklahoma,* I might have looked like I was practicing a tricky bit of choreography.

When I reached the front door, I took a deep breath and closed my eyes. This was it. Nona had prayed with me before I left, asking God to order my steps. Thinking of Nona and her sweet, almost conversational way of praying made my throat tingle and my eyes sting, even closed. Nona talked to God like he was holding her hand. She didn't even fill all the silences with words but let the spaces draw out, comfortable and worn, unhurried like a tide's arrival or departure. I loved listening to her and had thanked her for her prayer that morning. "Strong and courageous," she'd said. That's what I was supposed to be, with God's help.

I knocked on the door, and the woman who answered summoned up every weak and uncourageous feeling to the marrow of me.

"Yes?" She spoke with a heavy accent, eyes halved into wary half-moons.

"Hello. Or *guder mariye*. Afternoon, I mean." I cleared my throat. "I'm Professor Moss's assistant."

"Professor Moss?" the woman repeated. She looked to be closing in on seventy years. Mother would have recommended a wrinkle cream, but something told me this lady would not have been a willing guinea pig. She stood at least three inches shorter than me but might as well have been Goliath. Her hair was pulled back into a skin-numbing bun contained by a starched white bonnet. I could almost feel the pull of the comb as I looked at her.

"Sonya Moss? The professor who comes to cook with you on Tuesday afternoons?"

The woman appeared to be considering my words, rolling through the old noggin, trying to put a face to Moss.

"Tall, skinny, very pale?" I made a pinched face and then tried my hand at Professor Moss's bark-laugh.

"Ahhh," she said, nodding. "The Moss. She is the horrible cook."

Another woman, half the Friendly Greeter's age, came to stand in the doorway. Her cinnamon-hued hair, also pulled into a bonnet, fell in accidental wisps around her face, which boasted an early summer's tan. She wiped her hands on an apron and took in my bonnet with round blue eyes. I'd like to think she was impressed, maybe a bit jealous of my style.

"May I help you?" She smiled at Friendly Greeter and said something in Pennsylvania Dutch or German or Pig Latin, none of which I spoke fluently. F. G. hobbled away but not before casting a disapproving glance in my direction.

"I'm here to take Professor Moss's place," I said. "She's very busy with her writing and teaching and brooding and asked if I might take over her research project with you all." My thoughts flashed to when I'd pushed the fake Dear John note under Moss's office door and spied on her through the window. Her face had fallen as she read it, so disappointed that the Schrock family had decided to take a break from their cooking sessions with her. God willed it, they'd said, which might have been a teeny bit of blasphemy on my part, but it *was* inarguable. Not a peep of protest from the professor, and on the Schrocks' front porch I stood.

"Yes, that will be fine," the woman said. She held out her hand and offered a warm smile. "My name is Sarah Schrock. You met my mother-in-law, Mary Schrock. She is the one who talks to Professor Moss."

I nodded and kept smiling. Friendly Greeter was to be my primary source? I followed Sarah through a simply appointed living room and toward the back of the house. Not the sweet, plump gray-hair I'd pictured, Friendly Greeter was Granny Schrock. No worries, I told myself as we entered the kitchen. She'd warm up to me.

Mary sat on a chair at a long wooden table, putting a metal potato peeler to a carrot with such vengeance, I cringed.

Sarah pointed to an empty chair next to her mother-in-law and then left my side. Soon she had her back to me at the kitchen sink. Two young girls busied themselves around the large room, one sweeping, one leaning over the countertop, sleeves rolled up and kneading bread. Willowy and fair, the kneader looked up at me and smiled quickly before returning to her work.

"You are the new professor?" Granny said, not looking up.

"Yes, I am. I mean, no, I'm not a professor. But I'll be pretending I am." I took a breath. This woman was unraveling me, that's what. "I'll be taking Professor Moss's place for a while. She says she's sorry she's too busy to come."

Granny pushed out a chair with her foot. "Sit."

I sat, tucking my feet under the chair.

"Today we peel." She passed me a peeler and a bowl of vegetables. "You watch." She looked at me, eyes half-moons again, as if she, too, had read that online article about eye slits and interrogation. She placed her veiny hands deliberately, one holding the carrot, one gripping the peeler. "Start at top, peel to down. Straight line." She moved the peeler downward at a pace better suited to microscopic surgery. Oh, glory, was she slow. I watched for the first three centimeters but darted my eyes over to the others in the room. I thought I heard a giggle, but no one met my gaze.

"You are watching?" Granny said, rapping one bony knuckle on the table.

I jumped and said, "Yes. Every move!"

"Because," she said, marking the *s* sound, "I do not teach a girl who will not listen. *Ya, maed?*"

"Of course, Grandmother Mary," Sarah answered. The other girls made mewling noises in agreement.

"English girls do not learn to cook." Granny resumed her peeling. "I have been told that they eat nothing but sugar and alcohol and bacon." She looked at me with eyebrows arched but didn't seem to want a response. Matt would be so pleased to hear this rumor. "But at this house, we eat all of God's bounty. You need not much added if the ingredients are simple and good."

"Right," I said, eyes glued on my first carrot. "Simple and good."

"This is the key to a good life, pleasing to God and His perfect will." Granny settled back in her chair, and I thought I heard the kneader sigh. "Simple life, not burdened with too much. You English like too much of too much." She pointed her peeler at me. "Too much money, too much houses, too much cars, too much fast running from place to place. Our people separated from this, thanks be to God. And look how happy we are." She gestured to the other women. Sarah returned a dutiful smile and approached the table with a glass of water.

"Would you like a slice of bread? The first two loaves are almost done."

Oh, the bread. I'd hoped she was going to ask. I'd eaten lunch, but not much of one because of nerves and because of the time it took to coax the hair into a bun. The smell of baking bread had enveloped me in the living room and tempted me from that moment onward.

"Yes, I'd love some. Thank you." I took a sip of water. "The smell is wonderful."

Sarah blushed slightly. "You are kind."

Granny Mary sniffed. "Man does not live on bread alone. And this bread is not the most impressive. My daughter Grace is excellent bread maker. She lives in Pennsylvania with her thirteen children."

I think I was supposed to be impressed with this obscene number because Mary prompted me.

"Thirteen children, none of them dead."

"Oh, wow." I said. "That's really great."

Sarah bit her bottom lip and hustled over to the oven. I watched her slide two loaves out of jet-black baking pans, seeing from her ease how second nature the act was to her. I felt the kneading girl's eyes on me and turned my head to meet her stare. She cocked her head and smiled slightly until the other girl poked her ankles with the broom to sweep below her feet. The girls laughed softly and exchanged what sounded like playful banter. I, for one, was feeling sorry for myself that a score of five on the AP Spanish exam was getting me nowhere.

"Your name is what?" Mary pounded her fist once on the tabletop. I jumped. Table pounding seemed an excessive use of theatrics to get my attention, but no one else in the room skipped a beat.

"My name is Nellie. Nellie Monroe." As the words left my mouth, I wanted to groan at my own stupidity. What PI reveals her given name? I'd even decided beforehand to be known as Ruth Ford, my own little shout-out to Harrison and his work with the Amish. That Mary woman, though. I just couldn't settle into myself with her around.

"Look, Nellie Monroe." Mary poked my cutting board with the end of her peeler. "You have peeled more carrots than the skinny professor did in all her time with me."

I let my eyes fall to the board, now laden with a pyramid of peeled carrots.

Her eyes sparked, and I thought I saw remnants of a mischievous girl. "Next time, we chop."

She rose slowly from her chair.

I followed suit and waited while Mary scrutinized my face. Finally she spoke.

"Next week Tuesday. Do not be late."

I nodded. "Got it." I took her hand and curtsied for emphasis. "Good-bye."

I could feel them watching me as I left, but I kept my bonnet up and strode right through the house to the front door. Amish 101, first session, and I was already skipping to the top of the class.

11
Better Left Unsaid

Nona was naked when I got home. I'd called up the warning greeting, but she didn't answer. With worry nudging my feet to climb the stairs even faster, I burst open the door to the attic and found her naked and dancing to Al Green.

"Good gravy," I said, one hand flying up to my face far too late. That kind of image sears within milliseconds. "Nona!" I shouted through my fingers. "Lots of flesh. Pale, fleshy flesh, Nona. Sorry. I'll come back." I turned back toward the door, but she called over the music.

"Don't be such a prude, Nellie Augusta Lourdes." She must have turned down the volume because Al kept singing but more softly. "I couldn't hear you over my music. Don't you just *love* disco funk? Nellie, turn around, for Pete's sake. I have my robe on."

I turned slowly, hand still over my face.

Nona laughed. "Naked I came into the world, and naked I will return." She shook her head at me. "You're worse than Mrs. H. It's not like you haven't seen breasts before."

"I tend to keep my breasts to myself."

"That'll change soon enough," she said. The singsong voice was particularly disturbing—one should not discuss breasts in singsong.

"Not likely," I said, following her to the window chairs. "Unless you have plans for bringing back arranged marriages." I twisted my body in the chair and draped my legs over one of its high arms. "I just got back from my first day on the job."

She sat primly down, all decorum now that she was clothed. "How was it?"

I took a moment before answering. "Not exactly fast-paced, but not a disappointment either. I met some interesting people."

She nodded. Her eyes were clear and bright, no sign of the shadows that often clouded them. "Any of them men?"

"Goodness." I sounded huffy. "What's with the man focus today? I'm trying to tell you about my first day of a *career.* Women's rights, remember? Independence? Freedom from oppression? Shattering the glass ceiling?"

"I've always thought that was a tragic metaphor." Nona shook her head mournfully. "What a beautiful image, a ceiling made of glass! Why on earth would anyone like to break it?"

"I think the idea is that equality in the workplace is really a mirage—"

She interrupted me with a toss of her head. "Rubbish, and you know it. Who cares if you break through every ceiling in the world, glass and otherwise, if there's no one on the other side to share it with?"

I stared at her face, flushed with emotion, and couldn't stop the smile. "Nona, I have to say. I love to see you fiery." I pulled my legs down from the chair arm and leaned across the space between us.

Gripping her soft hands in mine, I said, "You're the best thing going in this house, you know that?"

She looked at our hands, holding tightly to each other, and her eyes filled. She drew a shaky breath and said, "Sometimes it's harder to know things are falling apart." Her eyes found mine. "I know things are falling, Nellie. I wish it weren't so, but I know it all the same."

I brushed tears from her face, right cheek first, left cheek, back and forth as she needed. For many slow minutes we sat together in the waning light of afternoon, I comforting my clear-eyed grandmother with nothing but silence and shared heartache.

"I'm glad you had a good day, honey." She patted my hand, tears still forging quiet rivers down the wrinkles in her cheeks.

"Me too," I said, lowering my forehead to touch hers. "I'm glad you had a good day too."

The next day was my day off from Tank's, and I planned to bury myself in Amish reading. In addition to the doorstop Professor Moss gave me, I'd cleaned out the Casper Public Library. The librarian, Mrs. Fredricks, had long since stopped initiating small talk with me, the last straw being in fifth grade when I'd asked her fifteen consecutive questions she was unable to answer. She'd pursed her lips at the end of that interaction and hadn't pried them open in my presence since.

Even with her sourpuss attitude, however, Mrs. Fredricks knew the library's collection better than any old broad there. She'd mutely pointed out every single book in the building having to do with the Amish, including a racy romance series with bonnets and suspenders flying all over the covers. I'd taken one of those for good measure, which had made Fredricks pinch all the blood out of both upper and lower lips.

On my bedroom desk sat the bodice ripper, the book from Moss, a memoir from a woman who left the Amish, and two histories that looked dry enough to start fires. I'd also picked up an Amish cookbook in Git 'n' Go, our local convenience store. A strange place to procure reading material, I admit, but I'd put it right on top of my bag of Twizzlers and heard from the cashier I was the first to buy a copy since she'd started working there two years ago.

By nine, I was halfway through the bodice ripper when I heard a tentative knock on the door.

"Come in," I said, knowing it had to be my mother. Pop had been scared of my bedroom since I'd entered sixth grade. Mrs. H. was categorically opposed to my privacy and would never have knocked, and Nona preferred putting her nose right into the doorjamb and singing, "Yoo hoo! Party's here!"

Sure enough, Annette turned the knob and poked her head in. "Hello, dear," she said, stepping gingerly over the threshold. She clicked over to me in red heels and pecked me on the top of the head. At least, I think she did as I heard the demure smack of lipsticked lips and smelled a waft of her perfume. I didn't have the heart to tell her I hadn't actually felt this traditional greeting since I was a bald baby, as the afro simply could not be penetrated by something that polite.

"How are you?" I said. I turned around in my desk chair and watched her take an inventory of the room.

She picked up a stuffed bear that was missing one eye. "Perhaps it's time for a childhood intervention? This room could use a grown-up touch, don't you think?"

I shrugged. "I'll get to it. Not at the top of my list, though." A younger, less mature Nellie might have pointed out the lunacy of a mother entering her daughter's bedroom once a quarter and dishing out tips on domesticity, but the more mature Nellie prevailed. "Where's Pop?"

She moved a pile of clothes to make room on my bed for her sculpted tush. "I believe he's golfing with Tank. I've learned it's best for me to steer clear of their boy outings." She wrinkled her nose. "Even in their fifties, those two spend most of their time together discussing flatulence and football."

I caught my breath. Annette had said *flatulence* without blushing. This from the woman who'd told me women had babies through their earlobes and that's why they wore earrings. "Mother, such language!"

"Oh. Sorry," she seemed genuinely surprised that I'd noticed. "I guess sometimes I forget I'm supposed to be maternal." Her fingers smoothed the bear with one eye. "You've always been rather self-sufficient, you know."

I bit my lip, worried about her sad smile. Annette was supposed to be the unfeeling one in our family. Sad smiles would really mess up that balance. "I suppose I learned from you. Don't strong women beget strong daughters?"

She laughed. "Is that what I am? A strong woman?" She took a deep breath and held her chest high as she let her lungs release all the oxygen. She stared at my *Law and Order* poster but didn't seem to see anything on it, which was a shame because Mariska Hargitay looks particularly intimidating. After a moment, she said, "What are we going to do about Nona?"

I bristled. "Nothing. Everything, I mean, but just like we have been doing."

She turned to me. "She's worse, Nellie."

"Of course she is," I said. I stood and started folding the clothes on the floor, which should indicate how distressed I was. "You and Pop only come around every few months, which is an eternity when you're eighty-two years old."

My mother's spine stiffened. "Now, don't make this about me."

"I'm not," I said into a rumpled sweatshirt, not wanting to look her in the eye. "But you better not either. Don't make this into something it's not, just because you're surprised every time you come home. I'm doing … *we're* doing fine. Mrs. H. gives her all her medicines like clockwork. Either she or I is with Nona at all times, and we watch her way more closely and with more love than any ridiculous, life-depleting old people's home would." I stopped, out of breath. My scalp prickled with tiny beads of sweat.

"Nellie." She stood and came to me. She put one hand on my shoulder, which probably meant she wanted me to hug her. I stood still and waited.

"Honey, she's going to need help we can't give her here."

"We're her family." My voice sounded small.

"Yes." She paused. "What's that on your desk? Nellie, are you reading dime-store romances?" She started to giggle. "I'm sorry. I know this may not be the moment, but *that* book on *your* desk is the funniest—" She broke off into hard, almost painful fits of laughter.

Watching her made my body relax. In fact, I started to laugh myself. "It's kind of a long story."

"No, no," she shook her head. "Please don't explain it to me. I'm thrilled, really." She laughed again, clutching her stomach. "You memorized a monologue from *Othello* when you were ten! Janice Thompkins used to make snide comments about.... But here you are, and it's like ... backwards maturation!"

Now, honestly, it wasn't that funny. If you'd walked into my bedroom at that moment, you would have thought that we were a few peas short of a casserole. Mother rolled around on my bed, gripping her skinny ribs, and I leaned on my wall for support. It occurred to me in those moments that parenting me must have presented its own challenges for Super Annette. I let her laugh, let her think I was into pretend literature, let us both postpone the reason for her quarterly visit. I handed her a tissue to wipe her eyes and knew some things could wait.

12

New and Improved

Amos leaned against the counter and tipped back a can of Red Bull. I didn't point it out, but he had no business ingesting more sugar.

"Have you tried this Red Bull Energy Drink?" His eyes bulged. "It is the best way to work! I finished two frames yesterday morning."

"Yes, and such clean, straight lines." The frame on the third hole looked like a four-year-old had held the nail gun.

"Exactly, this is true." He nodded, marveling at his own ability. He used his shirt to wipe beads of condensation off the bottom of the can. "And you like this new shirt, am I correct?"

It was a short-sleeved button-down, and if I wasn't mistaken, contained shoulder pads. "It's very bright." Neon green with splatter paint.

"This is the secret," he said, gesturing for me to lean in. "This is a shirt that will *glow in the darkness.*"

"You don't say."

"Yes, I say it. I found it on the for-sale rack in the back of the Walmart. The tag said it would glow in the darkness, and when I got home, I found this to be true advertising!" He grinned and toasted my imaginary can of Red Bull before taking another swig.

I cleared my throat. "So my first afternoon at the Schrocks went well."

He nodded and watched my face. "You met her?"

"Granny Schrock? Sure I did."

"She can destroy humans."

"Doubt it." I sniffed. "She was a pussycat with me. I'll have answers for you in no time."

Amos shook his head. "This is difficult for me to believe, but I am happy to be observing. I am only glad she will not be talking to *me* for hours each Tuesday. When I was a young boy, I heard the news that she bound up small children in her attic and made them memorize all of the New Testament before she let them go."

"I'll brush up on the Good Book, just in case."

He raised his eyebrows. "You are laughing, but you do not know very much. I lived near that woman my whole life. You have just met her." He poked a finger at me. "To say the words of this amazing Mr. T, I pity the fool."

"What happened to *Gidget?"* I opened up the cash drawer to get a count before the day began.

"I finished her. Now I watch *A-Team.* It is magnificent."

The front screen door creaked open, and Matt entered.

He fist-bumped Amos. "How's it going?"

"It goes very well, thank you," Amos said. He held up his beverage. "I would like to buy you a can of the Red Bull Energy Drink."

Matt raised an eyebrow. "Thanks, dude, but it might be a bit early for me. I usually start my energy drink IV at nine. We're an hour shy of that mark."

Amos was already stationed in front of the vending machine, quarters flying. "Do not worry about the time," he called back. "You will not notice the hour once you have swallowed your first taste."

"Wow," Matt said in lowered tones. "Neon suits him."

I sighed. "Believe me, it loses its charm by noon. What are you doing here?"

He folded over the counter and pushed his nose on the glass top. "You know, Nellie, there are kinder ways to phrase a greeting. How about, 'It's lovely to see you, Matt. You are so handsome, I find myself breathless in your presence'?"

"I was getting to that."

Amos returned, bearing two cans of Bull. He handed one to Matt and turned to me. "This is for you, Nellie. I know you will be grateful for it later in this day."

"Thanks, Amos," Matt said. "How's the mini-golf project? Tank pimping you out to other parts of the course yet?"

Amos nodded gravely. "The mini-golf is going well. But I am not certain about the pimping. Is this a verb? Is it like our talk at the diner, Nellie?"

Matt finished a swig of his can and met my glance. "You guys went to Frank's?"

"Have you been there?" Amos began to sway back and forth, far too quickly to, say, calm a baby but just the right speed if you're drinking liquid SweeTarts. "Have you eaten their very cold ice-cream malt shakes? I had—what, Nellie? Three? They are wicked good."

Matt watched my face. I felt my cheeks getting red, which was nothing if not irritating. "What?" I said, flustered. "Can't a girl go out with a boy without weighing in with you?" Definitely not the way I heard it in my head first, but I didn't like feeling cornered. Private investigating was private, and Matt was going to have to learn to accept that.

"Totally," Matt said. He took a long sip before coming up for air. He drew back and pitched the empty can into the trash, two yards away.

"This is a great shot!" Amos said. "You are an athlete *and* a technological resource. I admire this."

"How's the new job?" Matt was staring at me, which, last I heard, was socially inappropriate.

"You have a new job, Nellie?" Amos's eyes bugged. "Where? What about the Tank job?"

"No, no," I said, shaking my head. I gave Amos what I hoped was a meaningful glance. "He means, just the … *that* job."

It took a moment, but the light dawned. "Ahh," Amos said. He made a cutting motion by his throat. "You do not need to be saying another word."

Matt watched this exchange, his mouth opened slightly. "Sweet," he finally said. He slapped the counter with both hands. "Well, I should be going. Have to work at ten." He began walking backward toward the door. "Thanks for the drink, Amos. Nellie, maybe I'll see you around? Maybe not, though. I'm pretty busy lately."

"I love it when our plan will be coming together," Amos called, pantomiming a fist bump in the air.

"Bye," I said, watching Matt go. He didn't look back, and I heard him rev his Chevette before taking off down the gravel driveway.

I careened into the parking lot of A Cut Above at exactly four thirty-five. Tossing my keys into my purse and slamming the door, I booked it to the front entrance, hoping Mrs. H. wouldn't hear about this. The bells above the door announced my arrival, making everyone in the salon turn toward me.

"Hey, everybody," I called, long aware of the social mores in such a Casper moment. Ignoring the stares was tantamount to disrespect, even though my arrival at a hair appointment was really none of their darn business. Maybe in Cleveland no one would care when Nellie did or did not get her hair cut and whether or not she was a tidge late.

"Hey, honey," Bette called from the last chair of three facing a half-wall of mirrors. "I'll be right with you. Almost done with Kitty here."

I signaled no hurry, relieved that Maud, the salon owner, would not feel the need to call Mrs. H. about my tardiness since Bette was running late anyway. Maud and Mrs. H. were friends, I supposed, though I couldn't for the life of me imagine any warmth emitting from either of them. She stood at the chair closest to the door, rolling a tight perm into the short blue hair of Mrs. Clancy O'Malley, a woman who owned twenty-three cats and counting. I waved to Maud, who nodded upward with her double chin and left me at that. Again with the warmth.

I took a seat by the magazine rack and began a halfhearted page-through of *InStyle.* Most of the models seemed about my age, and they were female. Other than that, though, I could find very little that connected me to them. I saw heavy representation of eye makeup, heels, and some horrible phenomenon called "skinny jeans," but no one who looked like me. Then I turned to a story titled "I Hate My Hair! What I Did to Tame My Mess." Now, *this* girl looked like me, at least in the "before" photo. She was white and had a blonde Brillo pad around her head that looked a lot like mine. I stared at her, stared at her happy, "after" photo, and felt the first twinges of girliness I'd had in years. When Bette came up front to settle Kitty's bill, I slammed shut the magazine, feeling hopeful and silly in equal parts.

"You take care now, Miss Kitty," Bette said, patting the woman's arm. "You tell that Howie he needs to take a girl out when she looks this fresh and pretty."

When the door shut behind Kitty, Bette turned to me and clapped her hands. "All right, darlin'. I'm ready for the mane."

I tucked the magazine under my arm and allowed myself to be side-hugged by Bette.

"How are things, girl?" She used a firm grip to tuck a strand of hair behind my ear. After years of trimming my hair, the woman knew how to be a disciplinarian.

"I'm all right, thanks." I put my purse under the mirror.

She stared at it. "Well, isn't that something," she said. "I don't believe I've seen a denim purse for a good long while." She smiled at my reflection in the mirror. "You march to your own beat, don't you, Nellie Monroe? I like that."

I looked at the purse, a gift from my mother in junior high. I suppose that qualified it for outmoded, but I couldn't see why I'd buy a different one. Not really one for purses in general, this one suited my needs. It held a wallet, an elastic for my hair, and a tube of Mary Kay lip gloss, the same one that had been in the purse the day I received it as a thirteenth-birthday present. Compact and utilitarian. Exactly what a purse should be.

"If denim's out," I said to Bette, "what's in?"

She bit her lower lip, stifling a giggle. "First off, women now prefer purses that can hold more than a chipmunk." She shook her head. "Oh, how my dear and frugal husband would prefer that I still carried a denim purse from the early nineties."

"You can have mine," I said, shrugging. "I'll even include the chipmunk."

She laughed, showing two rows of white teeth with three silver fillings in the back. She pulled a black cape around my front and snapped it at the nape of my neck. "Now, miss," she said, "what are we doing with this hair today? Standard trim and all-over thin?"

I cleared my throat and cast a nervous glance toward Maud, who, predictably, was silent and listening to our conversation. Mrs. Clancy O'Malley had fallen asleep in the cloud of perm fumes.

"I ..." I began, then lowered my voice to a near-whisper. "I think I'd like to try something different." I pulled the magazine out from under the cape and pointed to the makeover story. "Can you do that to me?" I whispered.

Bette read in silence for a moment. Maud glanced up from the rollers to see what all the hush was about.

Closing the magazine and placing it carefully on her station counter, Bette turned to face me. "I've been waiting for this moment for eight years. And the answer is yes, I can do that to you." She took a deep breath and closed her eyes. "I thought you'd never ask."

I thought she was being dramatic, but it turned out that Bette *had* actually been pining for me to do something about my hair for eight years. Once I opened the floodgates, the woman was on a tear.

She stabbed a stack of foils and peeled one off the top with the end of a comb. "I mean," she said, her breathing shallow, "the options are really endless. I know you were burned by that around-the-state quest your mom took you on all those years ago. But hair has come *so far* since then. There are straightening techniques that we didn't even *know* about in the late nineties, the whole flatiron revolution, entire lines of products specifically designed for women of color."

"Or white girls with kinky hair."

"Exactly!" She nodded, her face gravely serious. "And these auburn low lights we're putting in are going to make your natural color shine but in a sophisticated way. Because you're a woman now, Nellie. You have to remember that."

Ew. I hoped this wasn't going to head into a discussion of fallopian tubes, because even though I still carried a chipmunk purse, I knew all about the Miracle of Life.

"And let's say you want to go curly," Bette continued, happily distracted from my womanhood. "Curls are *very* in. I have lots of ideas on how to manage your curls without giving in to frizz."

I watched her pull strand after strand of my hair out from its nest and gently brush on blue goop. I was on the cusp of starting my career and having real-life clients and real-life business cards.

I needed to inspire confidence in my capabilities and if low lights would help with that, I was open.

"Time to cook." Bette patted the foils, and we looked at my reflection.

"Have mercy," I said. By layering the foils on my already wild coiffure, Bette had created a full metallic-tinged circle around my head. I looked like one of those Renaissance saints on the walls of museums, orbed with my modern extraterrestrial halo and full of holy fear.

"Don't worry," Bette said, steering me toward a fancy-looking dryer mounted to the wall. "This is only the first step. The first step is always the most difficult."

I'd heard that said about drug rehab but not as much about hair. After a good twenty minutes "cooking" and a vigorous shampoo, Bette led me back to her chair and started to cut. This part was familiar, and I relaxed as I filled her in on my family, work at Tank's, my plans for the summer.

Maud didn't even pretend she wasn't listening. "Hey," she called, "I heard there's an Amish out at the golf course. What's he like?"

"Um, nice, I suppose," I said. Bette looked at me so hard, I broke eye contact. I would *really* need to work on my skills of deception. The nuance was killing me.

"I see," Bette said, drawing out the words. "Like what kind of nice? Personality nice, or nice-to-old-lady-golfers nice, or nice-to-look-at-shirtless nice? Or all three perhaps, you lucky girl?"

Maud's cackle woke Mrs. Clancy O'Malley from her slumber. She laughed too, as if she hadn't missed a word.

"Just nice," I said, trying for a breezy, disinterested tone. "I guess he's good-looking, but I'm not interested."

"Ah, hard-to-get." Bette nodded and snipped off an alarming amount of hair. "The oldest but most effective game in the book. Be careful, Nellie, because if you're good at hard-to-get, you just might land yourself a husband."

Maud snorted. "Better hope he won't turn you Amish. Those people are bizarre." She said the word as if trying to impress me. Two syllables with a French derivative must have been big to Maud. She raised an eyebrow and nodded at me, I guess waiting for applause.

"*I* heard," Bette offered in a stage whisper, "that they don't let their children bathe but one time a month."

"That's true," Mrs. Clancy O'Malley said. "I read it once. And they also don't allow women to speak in public. Not even at funerals, bless their hearts."

"Well, I should say." Maud clucked her tongue. "It's no wonder they don't want electricity. Probably worried the word would get out about their *repressive* ways." More staring at me, nodding, upping the ante with three syllables.

"Actually," I said, trying really, really hard not to roll my eyes or make scoffing noises, "the Amish typically bathe once a week, which is plenty but strange to the average American, who consumes more than twice the world's average of water any given year, roughly the volume of an Olympic swimming pool. Also," I continued, feeling my heart beat faster, "women are encouraged to speak, both privately and publicly. Typically, though, they do it with more dignity and kindness than we do. And as for electricity, they've chosen to separate themselves from what they perceive as a rushed and empty culture. Instead, they cut themselves off from any technology that might put a distance between themselves and their families, the land, or God.

Admirable, really." My *face* needed low lights by this time. "I don't think I'd have the discipline to live that way."

Silence descended on the salon. A swollen bubble of air rose in the water cooler.

Bette cleared her throat. "So he's hot?"

Maud slapped her thigh and made it jiggle while Mrs. Clancy O'Malley giggled into a handkerchief.

"Whatever," I said into Bette's belly. She stood in front of me, snipping final touches in long bangs around my face but shaking from laughter. "Just don't mess up my hair while you're laughing at your own jokes."

"Come on, now," she said, spinning my chair to face the mirror. "What will the Amish boy say about this?"

I stared at myself. It wasn't like the movies where the woman turns to the mirror weeping and telling everyone how in love she is with herself. But, holy cats, did I look great. Bette had taken up the length to just below my shoulders and had cut soft layers all the way around. My hair was still curly but the curls were loose and boingy. Forgive me, Merriam-Webster, but they were boingy. I turned my head back and forth and was happy to see my hair move, despite a sprinkling of hair spray Bette rained down.

"Wow," I finally said. "Bette, you're a genius." I met her eyes in the mirror and grinned. "Why didn't you do this years ago?"

"Shut up." She bit her lower lip and reached for a tissue to blot her mascara.

I stood to go. "Bette, please. The drama is too much."

"I can't help it," she said, her voice sounding all snotty and stuffed up. "Beauty makes me cry. It's my artistic temperament!"

I shook my head, feeling my curls bounce on my shoulders, and straightened my spine as I walked. One solid client and a new haircut, and I already felt a successful career knocking at my door.

13

School of Hard Knocks

I stopped at the threshold of the back door and listened. Robust soprano and alto voices mingled in an upbeat hymn. It was not yet noon, but the June sun beat bossy rays onto my bonnet, probably doing untold damage to my new hairdo. I squinted through the curtains, sweat prickling my scalp. During a break in the singing, I knocked twice on the glass. Sarah came to the door and peeked through the curtains.

"Hello, Nellie," she said when she opened the door. "We are pleased to have you visit again. Come in." She stood aside to let me pass.

I smiled and stepped into the kitchen, which was imperceptibly cooler than outside. The scent of yeast hung heavily in the air, but no heat came from the oven. The two young girls were there again, and the tall one approached me.

"How do you do?" She put out her hand for a shake. "My name is Katie Lapp. I help the Schrock women with household duties."

"No way!" I said and did a fist pump. The women stared, and I became all nonchalance. "I mean, great to meet you, Katie. I'm Nellie." Katie Lapp! *The* Katie Lapp! *God bless Professor Moss, and may she never know it!*

She laughed. "This I know, of course. You're the only English girl who comes to cook."

The shorter girl called over from the table, where she was folding napkins. "Nellie Monroe, I am Elizabeth Schrock."

"My only daughter," Sarah said. "Five boys and one girl, thanks be to God. All blessings but not many girls, so Katie works for us to help feed and clean after all the men."

"Girls!" Granny shuffled into the room, probably on her way back from pulling out the toenails of children. "Idle hands are the Devil's playthings!" She watched the women get back to their work and tilted her chin at me. "Nellie Monroe, you look tired."

"I do?" I slapped my cheeks for a bit of color, a trick I'd learned from watching my mother before she opened the door to guests. "That better?"

I heard Elizabeth giggle into her linens, but Mary brushed past me. "Follow." She walked quickly toward the kitchen table. "You have no reason to be tired. Sit down. When did you rise from your bed this morning?"

I took a careful posture on a kitchen chair. "Me? Um, not long ago, actually. We had a late night at my job last night and—"

"The hour."

The woman could use a lesson or two in finesse. "About eleven."

She threw back her head far enough for me to glimpse her uvula. "Eleven o'clock! Now ask me when I rose."

"Grandmother Mary Shrock, when did you rise?" I tried to sound inquisitive, but this was not my favorite way to communicate, having my lines read for me by a prompter.

"Four a.m. Each day, every day, each and every person in the Schrock family. I have been working seven and one-half hours at the time you open these pretty eyelashes." She poked the air near my head with one bony finger, snapping my gaze from Katie.

"Thank you," I said, but not before dodging to the right.

She narrowed her eyes. Beady eyes, by the way. "Why do you thank me?"

"You said I had pretty eyelashes. That's the nicest thing you've said to me."

"Pah," she said and wrinkled her nose. "You are lazy. How is that? 'Vanity of vanities, all is vanity.'"

"One of my very favorite Bible verses," I said. I smiled sweetly, counting the wrinkles on her cheeks in order not to lose sight of my gentler side. I was within spitting distance of *the* Katie Lapp, the goal of this entire project, but I had to bide my time before getting the information I needed from her. Granny was clearly the gatekeeper in this kitchen, and if I had to pretend I understood Ecclesiastes, then darn it, I would.

"Chop like this." Granny Mary took a knife that looked like it had been hewn from stone and pierced the outside layer of an innocent onion. She made a set of clean cuts once, then twice for a medium dice. Sniffing she handed me the knife. "You will not be very good at the first attempt. I have done this thousands of times in my life."

Sarah rummaged in a drawer and produced a newer-looking knife, which she held up. "Grandmother, this knife might be better for learning."

Mary threw an unimpressed glance over her shoulder. "My knife is fine. Work is good for all people, especially the lazy English." At this, she smiled, revealing a row of teeth that looked like they'd been shot in with a gun. When she saw me checking them out, she recovered quickly and clamped her thin lips shut once more. "Chop."

I took the next onion and peeled it slowly, acting dumbfounded that there were so many fascinating, eye-stinging layers. In general, I avoid looking dumbfounded and had no business trying to do so. Sure enough, after the second onion, I got distracted by Katie's conversation with Elizabeth. I leaned forward a bit in my chair, trying to make out their words, when Granny rapped the table sharply with her knuckles.

"What are you doing, Nellie Monroe? Do not waste food while you do not pay attention."

I looked down at the cutting board. I'd cut a thin slice off the side of the onion, contrary to the Mary Schrock Food Preparation Rules governing the universe. I sighed. Dumb wasn't going to work. "I like to cut them like this." I turned the onion onto its cut side, forming a good anchor for me to cut vertical incisions from top to bottom. In a swift motion, I cut another set of stripes horizontally and then finished with a neat dice, tossing the prickly head into the rubbish bowl at Granny Mary's elbow.

I took a moment to raise my eyes, fearful she would banish me back to my wayward people. Perhaps this was unforgivable, this assertion of a new idea. I mean, the woman had never used a hair dryer, so newfangled ideas on how to cut onions might be a bit off-putting.

When I finally looked up, her beady eyes were twinkling.

"*Gut,*" she said. "You are lazy, but you are not stupid. This I like." She shoved a heaping bowl of onions to my side of the table. "When we finish these, wc move to bread." Then, over her shoulder, she said something in rapid-fire Pennsylvania Dutch, which educed a round of laughter from the other women in the room.

Katie saw me frown. She called over to me in translation. "She says you are peacock, but a peacock is better than a pale mule from the university. Only she used a stronger word that I cannot repeat in English." They all laughed again, and I held out my hand to Grandmother Mary.

She shook it, mirth spilling out of her eyes. "Welcome, Nellie Monroe."

I grinned. An Amish potty mouth. Man, I loved my job.

I pushed the cart, and Nona held the list.

"Nectarincs," she said. "They're next." She held a pen poised above a yellow legal pad.

Mother and Pop had left for another tour of pleasure, this time to the Pacific Northwest for a smattering of golf tournaments and charity benefits. Nona and I had sat in the living room, watching the two of them fly back and forth through the house, packing everything from a faux fur stole for chilly nights (Mother) to a compass and camel pack in case the weather permitted a hike (Pop). Nona and I had happily munched on a bowl of popcorn, feeling it worthy of the cinematic entertainment offered right in our own home.

After the packing mayhem culminated in a histrionic good-bye—complete with Mother waving a hanky out the window of their departing Jaguar—I turned to Nona, who wore a bemused smile.

"Back to normal," I said, linking my arm through hers.

"Not to sound impudent, but thank goodness they're gone. It's like a long babysitting session when they come back, don't you think?"

I chuckled. "Only they're getting a bit wrinkled, so not as cute as babies. And Mother has sprouted a whole new crop of sun spots."

Nona gasped. "*Never* tell her that, Nellie. You know she'd be devastated. And your poor father would be on ice-pack duty for another round of tucking and nipping."

Despite my discouraging words about it, Nona watched cable sometimes when I was at work. I'd been able to cut her off from prime time's *The Bachelor* and *Hot or Not?* but my hands were tied when I left for the day. She referred to plastic surgeons on TLC by their first names: "Ted" disliked cutting right after working out, while "Margaret" hated men, particularly skinny men who came to her for calf implants.

After the farewell for Mother and Pop, we walked to the kitchen to prepare a grocery list to replenish our empty pantry. Nona wrote the list while I paged through cookbooks that would take advantage of summer produce. We were particularly excited about a recipe for grilled pork chops with blue cheese, fresh basil, and toasted pine nuts. As we shivered in the refrigerated air of TasteWay, Nona picked out ripe nectarines to grill and drizzle with honey.

"Hello, Mrs. Byrne." I was thinking of honey and its syrupy sweetness when Misty Warren-Pitz's voice greeted Nona in just such a tone, only grosser.

Nona turned. "Why, Misty. How lovely to see you." She smiled because Nona always smiles at those less fortunate.

"How *are* you?" Misty patted Nona's hand. "Everything going all right?" She cocked her head and a healthy application of purple eye shadow. "I heard *somebody* couldn't remember where she parked her car in our lot again the other day. You must be feeling *different* than usual."

"Boy, isn't that the kiss of death?" I was speaking too loudly. "Feels like just yesterday, doesn't it, Misty, when we were in junior high together, and you were torturing me for having the *different* kind of everything? Something about those *unusual* types that makes them such convenient targets."

"Nellie, honey," Nona said softly. "Bygones."

I stood with one hand on the cart, the other on my hip, feeling not one bit of joy in taking the low road. But I hadn't liked Misty's whiny implications, trying to coax from Nona some confession to pad any town rumors. I'd play Insult Volley with Misty Pitz if it meant Nona's privacy remained hers until the end.

Misty rolled her eyes. "No kidding, Mrs. Byrne. Honestly," she said, shaking her blonde mane that—now that my eye was trained—could use a touch-up on the roots. "When will you let that go, Nellie? We're grown women now."

I resisted the urge to ask just how her own *growth* was coming along but couldn't help glancing at her abdomen.

She noticed, and her face fell. "Gotta run, ladies. Great to see you both." She clipped off through the root vegetables, and Nona shook her head after the girl.

"I wouldn't trust that child farther than I could toss her," she said, "but you should still be nice, Nellie. Seven times seventy we forgive, you know."

"That makes four hundred and ninety, and I'm pretty sure I passed that milestone by sixth grade."

We walked slowly toward the bakery section. "I remember," Nona said, "when you used to come home crying every day after school."

I swallowed and picked up a loaf of sourdough.

"No one understood you, you'd say." Nona checked the bread off her list. "That wasn't quite true because I know you had Matt, for one. And me. And your mother and father."

I looked at her.

She giggled. "Okay, at least Matt and me."

I picked through the cheeses, muttering to myself about Gruyère, chèvre, Pecorino Romano, all in very poor French and Italian accents. *I don't come to the grocery store to relive junior high*, I thought. In Cleveland, I'd bet no one from junior high even surfaced in quotidian moments. Quotidian, from the Latin *quotidianus* for daily, mundane. Junior high was best lived once or never. If I ever had children, a rite of passage that wasn't high on the list, I'd home-school during junior high. That way, when they were shopping for zucchini and instead got a postcard from 1992—

"Oh, no." Nona's voice was small and scared.

I looked up from my burrowing. She stood in the middle of the aisle, her face etched with fear.

I dropped a wedge of cheese and hurried to her. "Nona," I said softly, forcing her to find my eyes with hers. "Nona, it's all right. I'm right here. It's Nellie. You're here. With me. We're getting groceries."

She watched my face.

I tried again. "You're in the supermarket with me. Nellie." I felt like sand had covered my throat.

After a moment, the fear receded behind specks of courage in her eyes. "TasteWay. Grilled pork chops and nectarines."

"That's right," I said. I gathered her small shoulders into a hug and blinked back any tears that threatened. Over Nona's shoulder, I saw Misty watching us. I steered Nona toward the front of the store.

"I don't really feel like grilling, do you?" I said. "What about take-out Chinese? We could stop at Happy Dragon on our way home."

"Oh, I love Happy Dragon," Nona said. We walked through the double doors. "I can't wait to read my fortune."

A warm wind pushed into us, making a loose and flying tangle of our hair, red and white, gripping each other at least for the moment.

14

Sincerely Yours

"Grass always looks softer than it feels." Matt slouched his torso toward the street, arms propped on his knees.

"You have your grumpy face on," I said around a bite of funnel cake. "The Fourth of July is a day of national joy, Matt."

He grunted and shifted position on the curb.

"You can throw on the grumpy face for Groundhog Day because it's built around the actions of vermin. Or Valentine's Day because it's capitalism-meets-Kenny-G, which is immoral." I blotted the corners of my mouth with a napkin. "But not July Fourth. Grumpiness on July Fourth is un-American."

He rolled his eyes, but I could see a smile forming against his will.

"Plus, we haven't seen each other all week, and you need to catch me up on your life."

The parade had started down by Bank of the Heartland and we could hear sounds of the Casper Senior High marching band as they rounded the corner a block down from us. We stood as the color guard passed, four men dressed in blues and carrying flags. Though cognitively I knew it to be impossible, I wondered if one of the men had fought in the Civil War, he was so stooped and ancient. I wanted to take his flag and carry it for him, but Matt assured me this would be a breach of military etiquette.

"Let him be a man," he said, and I thought I heard a note of snark in there.

I pulled a face. "I just want to help him. When I'm four thousand years old and carrying a flag for three miles in a parade route, I hope someone will come and help me carry it. Or would that not let me 'be a woman'?" I drew curt quotation marks with my fingers.

He shrugged. "No need for attitude, Lady of Liberty. I'm just saying the guy deserves a break. Guys, in fact, deserve a break."

I took a deep draw of strawberry smoothie and handed it to Matt. "Guys need a break," I repeated, watching a gaggle of Future Farmers of America pass in matching T-shirts and well-worn boots, throwing candy to the little kids along the route. "Yes, you're probably right. After years of repression and injustice, if there's one thing all white men need, it's a break."

"Dude!" he erupted. "Are you ever able to take anything seriously?" He turned to me and stared.

I cleared my throat, jerking my head to the people around us who had begun to follow our verbal sparring. "Sorry," I muttered. "I didn't know you felt so strongly about it." I slumped into my smoothie, which Matt had set down with a thud on the cement between us.

We didn't speak through the band's labored rendition of "Louie, Louie," the German Preservation League's wagon filled with plump blond people in *lederhosen,* or the parade marshal's car driven by Mrs.

Potts, my fourth grade teacher, and her husband. Mrs. Potts saw me from the car and started waving at a frenetic pace.

I waved back and caught a full-sized Butterfinger.

She winked and yelled, “Only for my favorite students!”

I broke off half and gave it to Matt.

“Thanks,” he said. “Sorry I blew up at you. I do think guys deserve a break from all you women,” he said, scowling. He took a big bite of the Butterfinger and chewed as he thought. “But mostly I think I’m sick of work. Don has been cutting everyone’s hours, and we’re only halfway through the summer. I’ve made enough for books and part of the first semester, but that’s it.”

Matt was one of six DuPage children, fifth in the birth order. This meant a lot of things that I envied, like camping in the backyard with more company than two Cabbage Patch dolls, holiday dinners where people competed to be heard, and enough people to play Capture the Flag in the woods behind their house without even having to call in reinforcements. It also meant, however, that everyone was on his or her own when it came to higher education. Matt’s mom had passed away when he was a toddler, and his dad was the nicest man around. He wanted his kids to do well, but on a bookkeeper’s salary, he had to cut the strings at eighteen.

“Why is Don dropping your hours? Is the Shack not pulling in the techies like it used to?”

We waved at a float sponsored by Riverside Electric. It was built to look like a dinosaur, though it looked more like a dehydrated purple frog with a tail. All along the hackneyed papier-mâché, employees had perched their sticky-mouthed children, none of whom was even interested in consuming candy anymore.

"Best Buy takes too much of our business," he said. "And online shopping. People in town can go lots of places now for what used to be available only at our store." He reached for my smoothie and glanced at me. "Nice hair, by the way."

"Shut up." I tucked a strand behind my ear. It had looked so easy when Bette had styled it in the shop, but I'd already had to call her once from my bathroom when I got halfway through blow-drying and it looked like I hadn't read the little warning about mixing electricity and water.

"Seriously. I like it."

I narrowed my eyes at Matt and was shocked to see him blushing. I punched him in the shoulder a little too hard.

"That was a compliment, you freak," he said, rubbing the welt. "Most girls would say thank you."

"Well, there's your problem." I cracked my knuckles. "I'm not most girls."

I could feel Matt revving up for a zinger of a comeback but was saved when the Casper Golf and Country Club tractor rolled into view. "That's Amos and Tank," I said and stood up to wave.

Matt pulled himself up to stand next to me. He brushed dirt off his rear and said, "I didn't know Tank owned a tractor."

"Just bought it," I said, still waving. "Said Amos made him want to reconnect to our agrarian past."

Matt turned his head to look at my profile. "Tank does not know the word *agrarian.*"

"True enough. I think his actual words were ''Bout time I got my HANDS on some MANURE!'"

Matt nodded. "That's what I thought." He made his index finger and thumb into a circle and let loose a whistle. Amos and Tank found us in the crowd, and Tank honked the tractor's horn, which sounded like a plane crash, only louder.

We groaned. Children on both sides of the street jumped, hands flying up to their scarred ears. The baby next to me started to cry.

"He got a deal," I said by way of explanation to the miffed mother. "The horn needs some work."

"Lookin' good," Matt yelled to Tank.

"Darn SHOOTIN'!" Tank yelled back. "God bless the USA, BABY!"

Amos waved from his perch in the driver's seat. He wore several layers of tank tops, all in camo print and a size too snug. He yelled, "This big rig can plow ten acres in ten minutes! It is not to be fathomed!"

I gave him a thumbs-up when he cranked "We Are the Champions" on the radio.

Matt and I watched them lumber past, scaring another set of children a block southward.

"Someone should tell Ye Olde Amish to use less gel in his hair," Matt said as we watched them recede. "It's starting to look painful."

I sat down on the curb again just as the middle-school scrapbooking club starting chucking Laffy Taffy from the back of a pickup. "It's growing on me," I said. "And it's not as spiky as it looks."

"What, you've touched it?" Matt caught a piece of strawberry taffy and started to unwrap it.

"I guess I have," I said, tipping my chin to think. "I can't place the exact moment, but I do know how it feels. Now, the DayGlo clothes and the tendency to practice club dancing in stores and restaurants—*those* things will need to stop. But change is slow, Matt." I swept my arm toward the bleachers. "If there's one thing this holiday teaches us, it's to be patient when a revolution is at hand."

Matt snorted, which I took as a prompt to continue speaking.

"For over two hundred years we've cultivated this dream called the United States of America, Matt DuPage, and still there are trials. Still there are burdens. Still there are struggles for freedom. And yet," I paused, index finger pointing skyward, "yet there is always hope. Hope for a new tomorrow, hope for victory in the wars we wage, hope that things will change for the better."

A silver-haired woman behind me poked me with the end of her umbrella. "Missy, if I have to hear one more word about hope, I'm going to be sick. I did *not* vote for Barack Obama, and you shouldn't have either." She sniffed and gave me another poke in the ribs.

I winced and turned back to Matt. "Did I ask for that?"

"Absolutely, you did," he said and finished off my funnel cake *and* my smoothie without even asking.

Mrs. H. was in rare form, even for her.

"Perhaps I should submit my request in writing, like an insurance claim." She beat the cushions on the living room couch until I thought they might start to bleed. "I could write, 'Dear Sir,' because I sure wouldn't use his given name."

I took a tiny scoop of pralines and cream out of my ice-cream dish, not wanting to hurry things along. "So," I said slowly, "you wouldn't write 'Dear Arthur DuPage'?"

She stared at me, stony-eyed and peeved, as she had for most of my childhood. "No, I would not. There are some words better left unsaid." She straightened her shoulders and looked off into the distance.

"Ah, self-righteousness. The linchpin of all dying relationships."

"Self-righ—! Dying!" She was sputtering.

I licked a slurp of caramel off my spoon.

"You listen here." Mrs. H. strode to my spot on the couch and pointed a Swiffer handle at my forehead. "If you knew what he did, you would not be calling me self-righteous. You'd be calling me"—she stopped and then the light bulb dawned—"a martyr! That's what! And second, this relationship is not dying. It's dead and gone and has been since 1969."

"Ooh, Summer of Love."

Mrs. H. looked at me with disdain. "Not all of us were hippies."

I squinted my eyes and tried to reframe Mrs. H. with fringed boots and long dingy hair.

"That was a good decision," I said. "So Arthur must have been a hippie. Is that why you're mad? He wanted you to smoke pot, but you were a good girl who wouldn't be caught dead with Mary and her Jane anywhere near your lips? You passed on grass? Said no to the giggle weed? No ganja, no griffa, no gunga? Wacky terbacky go home?"

I stopped, and she stared.

"Nellie Augusta Lourdes Monroe, you tell me the truth. Do you smoke marijuana?"

I let my head fall back on the couch cushions and sighed. When, oh, when would these people take me and my job as an *investigator of crime* seriously? If I didn't hone up on drug slang around here, who would?

"No," I said slowly. "I believe we were talking about you, Mrs. H. Listen." I put my bowl on the coffee table but returned it to my lap when I saw her glare. "After all these years, don't you think you'd feel better just telling someone what happened between you and He Whose Name Shall Not Be Spoken? Think of how much better you'd feel to let this secret out in the open."

To my surprise, she didn't leave the room. Instead she fiddled with the end of the Swiffer, seeming to consider my offer.

After a minute, I tried once more. "Forty years is a long time, Mrs. H."

She sat down carefully beside me. I scooted over to give her ample room, but she remained perched on the edge.

Clearing her throat she began. "I'll tell you. But." And she leaned over to grab my earlobe between two fingers. She pinched, and I whined. "You keep this to yourself, or I'll find ways to make you wish you had."

"Sheesh!" I rubbed my ear. "I'm twenty years old, Mrs. H. Do you think you could do away with the pinching?"

"We'll see," she said and leaned back slightly. "It's actually a short story. When I was in high school, Ar—he and I were friends. Good friends, really. We both played in the marching band, he on trumpet, I on clarinet."

"Cute."

"Not really. Arthur—I mean—" She shot me a look. "I'll use his name but only for the purposes of storytelling. After this, we go back to avoidance, got it?"

I nodded. "It's like when Prince didn't want a name but a symbol. Too cumbersome."

Confusion lighted on her face but was quickly dismissed. "So we played in band together, studied together, even went to a few dances together when we couldn't get other dates. The problem came during our junior year, the semester before I started going steady with Mr. H., God rest his soul."

I realize to the outside observer that referring to one's husband with a "mister" in front might seem a bit formal. But remember that this woman didn't use *any names at all* for people she didn't like. "Mister" was a term of endearment.

She smoothed her starched skirt. "That spring, Arthur started acting very strange. He wrote my phone number on the boys' restroom wall, and I got crank calls for a full month before the janitor repainted. He was dating a snotty girl at the time, Francine Waterson, who was beautiful and mean, a vicious combination in high school. She made me her pet project of irritation." She sat up primly and smoothed her skirt. "Francine was rather *developed,* whereas I was a late bloomer, so she used that difference between us as a point of ridicule." She looked over her spectacles at me, eyebrows raised.

I stared.

"What?" she said. "Didn't think I was in tune to those kinds of things just because I don't care to see you prancing about without a shred of modesty? Pshaw." She sniffed. "I tried talking with Arthur but he'd just laugh it off, tell me I was too sensitive. All this, though, all this I could have forgiven if he had stopped there. But he did not." Her eyes were large and sad, and all of the sudden I got a bit nervous. I knew it was my job to squeeze the truth from people, but maybe I should have left Mrs. H. alone. What if she were a part of a crime ring? What if she were running from the FBI, and we'd been harboring a fugitive for years without knowing it? What if she were actually a *man?*

"All this I could have forgiven." She took a deep breath. "But then Arthur asked me to go to our junior prom. I was surprised, seeing how he'd been practically humiliating himself to impress Francine. They'd broken up, was all he said. But I'd missed him. So I took him for his word and went to buy a dress." She held her hands together, grip firm, in her lap. "I'll never forget the way I felt in that dress. Empire waist with a satin sash, sky blue to match my eyes. There was a lace overlay on the bodice and it fell, all swishy, to the floor." She swallowed hard and then looked at me, almost as if she needed me to help her finish.

"What happened?" I asked softly.

She looked past me as she answered. "He never came."

I waited while the arrogant chirp of a blue jay pushed through the front porch glass.

"I stood in my bedroom, waiting for the doorbell so I could walk down the stairs in all my glory. Then I waited in the living room, watching out the front window. Then I waited on the front porch. I remember how my hair felt sticky with hair spray in the humidity and how my shoes started to ache, but I just stood until my daddy came out to tell me he'd be happy to escort me to the dance if I'd like."

I felt like a deflated balloon. All those years of wondering, and now I wished I couldn't see poor Mrs. H. in her 1969 prom dress, stood up and wilting.

"I found out that Monday at school that Francine had called at the last minute, and he'd taken her instead."

"Ouch," I said. *Bookkeeper gone bad,* I thought. Still, was it wrong that I'd hoped for something a bit more salacious? I mean, I *had* looked through microfiche in search of the answer to this mystery. I deserved the latitude to hope for something gritty, right? Maybe not the Witness Protection Program, but money laundering? White-collar crime? At the very least, an illegitimate child?

"It was very hurtful," she said, spine curved. "He'd been my friend for years, and all of the sudden, my feelings were less important than making a vapid girl laugh."

"What did you do?"

"I ignored him for the rest of high school. He called, he stopped by, particularly when Francine Waterson dumped him for Alan Nussbaum that summer. But I had none of it." She tilted her chin. "I was not a woman who forgave and forgot."

Atta girl, I thought. *Better to burn with resentment for the rest of your life.*

"And now," she said, pulling a stack of folded papers from the pocket of her skirt, "he won't leave me alone. Every morning, I find one of these dropped through my mail slot." She shoved them to me.

I opened the one on top. "Dear sweet, stubborn Lavinia," it read, "will we die with you mad at me? Love, Arthur." The second: "Lavinia, I still know you after all these years. And I'm still very, very sorry. Forgive me? I'm starting to grow long eyebrows, which means I'm on the down slope. Love, Arthur." The third: "Lavinia, remember when we skinny dipped in Crawford's pond?"

I looked up.

"I know," she said. She shook her head in dismay. "He's relentless."

"You skinny dipped with a boy in high school?" Unprofessional, I know, but it was a captivating image I was having a hard time shaking.

She pursed her lips and snatched back the stack of papers. "Well, I think that concludes our Dr. Phil moment of the decade. Don't tell anyone or else." She sounded much less menacing than at the start of our conversation.

My eyes followed her as she made her way to the dining room, dust rag at the ready yards before the archway.

"Thanks for spilling it," I called after her.

She raised her rag in salute without turning around.

I stood, and a splotch of white on the hardwood caught my eye. I opened it.

"Lavinia Loo," it read, "I won't give up, so *you* might as well. Yours, Arthur."

15

Field Work

"You're late."

Granny Mary stood behind the screen door to the kitchen and scowled.

"I'm sorry," I said. The leopard-print stockings stretched taut against my legs. I'd pulled them on in a hurry and could feel a twist of fabric that was acting as a tourniquet on my left leg. "I worked this morning and—"

Mary held up her hand. "It does not matter why, only that it is true. This is a good thing to remember in most situations." She waved me aside so she could open the door. "We garden today. The others are already there."

I fell into step beside her. "Gardening? As in outside?" My question came out like a lament. At twelve-thirty on a July afternoon, I'd already dreaded a kitchen cooled only by the stares of my instructor. A garden visit seemed better timed for, say, harvest. *Pumpkins*, I thought. *Let's wait for the pumpkins*.

"Church meeting was at our house Sunday. Sixty people came

and ate. We need to catch up on weeding, and you will help. Even English people who don't know anything can weed the plants. Maybe you do not eat plants, but you can weed them." At this, she dissolved into laughter. She slipped into Pennsylvania Dutch, sprinkling her laughter with phrases that were, apparently, much funnier than I could appreciate.

"Yeah, yeah, dumb English," I muttered. She was too busy with self-congratulation to hear me. We passed a barn with wide plank siding. A group of junior-high-aged boys stood in the mammoth doorframe. The black brims of their hats swiveled toward us. One of them smiled, but the rest just stared with mouths open.

Mary barked something fierce at them, and they went scurrying into the barn.

"What did you say?" I asked.

"The manure pile needs attention from boys who stare at women." She puffed up a bit, but I didn't have the heart to tell her they were probably more interested in me. For one thing, I was the only one in racy stockings, constrictive though they may have been. Also, my hair was pretty awesome that day, enough to dispel even the subtlest suggestion of Fraggle Rock. The key was copious amounts of product, more than I really want to describe here. Just know it was worth it.

We walked along a fence and got a healthy whiff of pig.

"Look, there are the new piggies." Granny Mary pointed. Strange, hearing a diminutive term from her. I decided to go with it.

"Oh, they're so cute," I said. "Look at their little snouts." In a pack, they came snorting and waddling over to us.

"*Nette schweine,*" Granny murmured. She petted one of them

through the slats of the fence. "My belly already rumbles to think of eating you, skin first."

"Mmm," I said through a frozen smile at little Wilbur. Granny rose from her haunches and kept walking. I mouthed "Sorry" as we left. I was no PETA member, but did she have to *describe* his death to him?

"Hello," she called as we rounded the corner behind a shed. Sarah, Katie, and Elizabeth straightened from their weeding stances and waved. It took a moment to make eye contact with all three of them because this garden was not the quaint patch Nona had tended for a few years when I was a kid. There, we could have reached out and touched each other at any distance within the plot. This monster, however, had the square footage of a Super Walmart. Sarah was knee-deep in sweet corn, planted all along the back border. Katie smiled at me from a good two hundred yards away, carrying a basket of green things amid other green things. I was too far away to make out what. And Elizabeth was closest to us, on her knees picking at the miscreants growing around a petunia border.

"Good grief," I said. "How many people does this feed?"

"Nine family members and a winter of company." Granny Mary's voice lilted with pride. "We grow raspberries, blueberries, and strawberries. Lettuce, spinach, and kohlrabi just for fun."

We walked toward Katie, who had kneeled carefully between two rows of peas.

"Green beans, lima beans," Mary continued, "carrots, potatoes, sweet corn, watermelon, muskmelon, onion, peppers, yellow squash, zucchini, tomatoes, rhubarb, and peanuts. Those are for fun purposes as well."

Crazy Amish. Always throwing kohlrabi and peanut frat parties. Fun!

"Katie," Granny said, "you will show Nellie Monroe how to weed around raspberries while you pick." She raised her eyebrows. "Keep your eyes watching her."

"Yes, Grandmother Mary," Katie said. She deposited her full basket at Mary's feet and picked up two empty galvanized buckets. She looped her arm through mine. "To the raspberries."

I smiled but stopped short when the granny cleared her throat.

"Thank you," I said quietly and tried looking depressed as Katie and I walked off together. When I thought we were out of earshot, I said, "I love raspberries."

"Shh," Katie said. She turned her head slightly and paused. "She listens and watches still. Wait to speak until I say."

We walked through rows of beans, their skinny Wicked Witch fingers poking our calves as we passed. Through a spot of lacy carrot tops and a jungle of rhubarb, we reached the easternmost border of the garden. Beyond us lay neat rows of soybeans, their leafy umbrellas nodding like debutantes in the warm breeze.

Katie turned, facing the way we'd come and what we could still see of Granny. I followed suit, squinting through the bushes. Granny Mary sat on a chair under an oak tree. She pointed at Elizabeth and issued an order in percussive Pennsylvania Dutch.

Katie giggled. "I am so happy she sent me with you. Poor Elizabeth. She will have two times the instruction. Here." She pointed to the plants, peppered with ripe fruit. "Pick the ones you would want to eat." She popped two in her mouth and grinned. "And eat as many as you like."

I pulled one off the vine. The berry was warm on my tongue, collapsing in a puddle of juice as soon as I bit. "Mmm," I said, shaking my head. "Awesome."

"Awesome?" Katie pulled off a handful and let them drop carefully into her bucket. "This means it is really great?"

"Right. Awesome, cool, fantab, dope." I didn't exactly know if anyone ever said "dope" anymore, but one look at Katie and her getup told me she wasn't exactly on the front lines of urban slang.

"Dope," she tried out the word slowly. "Raspberries are dope."

"These are," I said through a mouthful.

She laughed. "A few should go into the buckets." Her eyes were blue enough to merit mention in a Jane Austen novel. They matched her simple blouse and the expanse of sky that curved over us in a bright dome. Under her long skirt, bare toes peeked out.

I gestured. "How does Granny feel about that? Seems scandalous." I shimmied my skirt up above my knees and set to yanking my own stockings off as fast as I could.

She gasped and peeked through the branches. "Bare feet are fine when no men are around. Easier to wash off dirt and mud." She stepped back from the bushes. "But we do not lift up our skirts in public."

I tucked the leopard tights into my shoes. "Ah," I said, wriggling my toes. "I don't know how you do it, Katie. It is so stinking hot out here, and you're practically mummified in clothes."

She shrugged. "This is my normal custom." She nodded at my bonnet. "I do not wish to offend you, but that bonnet must make your head hot like a coal. Why do you wear it?"

I tugged at the strings and tossed the bonnet aside as well. "Out of respect, of course. Even the baby girls wear them in their strollers. Bonnets for all, I say."

She *tsk*ed. "Yours is too heavy. Can you even see side to side when it is on your head?" Concern knit her forehead. "It is awesome you do not trip more often."

I laughed, and she smiled. "All right. I'll leave it off when outside the eyeball range of Mary. And maybe you should consider shortening that skirt, at least in July and August."

She shook her head. "I tried wearing the tank tops and short pants for a spell, but they are not very comfortable."

I gaped. "Granny Mary let you wear tank tops and short pants?"

"Yes. No." She pulled off a rotting berry and tossed it behind her shoulder. "I wore those things during my *rumspringa*." She studied my face, thin eyebrows lifted in curiosity. "Do you know what this is? *Rumspringa?*"

Oh, did I. Just the past weekend I'd rented a DVD from the library about the time when Amish teens take off for a bit of oat sowing. Not all Amish communities were fans of *rumspringa,* but some, like Amos and Katie's, reasoned that by allowing youth to go buckwild on the "outside," they were better able to make an informed decision about returning to the Amish for good.

"I've heard of it," I said, waiting for her to tell me more.

"When I was sixteen years old, I was permitted by my family to test the world. We do this before deciding to be baptized as Amish." She moved a step away from me, having cleared the branches in front of her. "I know the Hollywood says *rumspringa* is a time of wild parties and drinking many kinds of alcohol beverages. But for me, I got bored quickly. The smoking makes me cough, and short pants are not comfortable to my body." She stopped, glancing at me. "I am talking too much."

"Not at all," I said. I walked behind her and began work on another section of berries. "I like to listen."

We worked in silence then, taking turns peeking through the branches to pinpoint Granny Mary's whereabouts. After a few minutes, I tried again.

"Did you date any boys during your *rumspringa?"* After a lifetime of people pronouncing my French middle name the same way they'd say the words *dog food*, I made special effort to get my German on.

She looked surprised or impressed; it wasn't immediately clear. "I did like a boy during that time. A boy from around here but different from all the others." She shook her head quickly, as if to clear out the cobweb of that thought. "That was two years ago. I do not know even where he is now."

My cell phone was burning a hole in my pocket. I could just imagine Amos's eyeballs popping out under his shellacked hairline when he heard Katie's voice on the other end. *But patience, my dear Monroe.* Cases were not solved in brash uses of technology with innocent Amish girls.

"What was he like, the boy?" I busied myself with watching the raspberries drop into my bucket. I thought I saw her shoulders slump.

"Kind, funny, a bit wild." She blushed. "Mostly kind. And he had very nice eyes."

It was true. Amos did have nice eyes. A bit over-enthused about nail guns, but he did have nice eyes. "He was Amish too?"

She nodded. "But now he is not." She let a handful of berries drop into her pail. "This is a serious problem."

I leaned into a gap in the bushes and saw Granny snapping the ends off beans. She was smiling. Dismemberment in any form, even vegetal, gave this woman pleasure.

I looked at Katie. "What did Grandmother Mary have to say about that?"

She smiled sadly. "She will not even say his name. No one will." She went back to work but her pace slowed. "His name was Amos. It is a good, strong name." At that, she stopped talking until we heard Sarah call us to break for lemonade and cinnamon cookies.

Katie swung her basket in a small arc by her side as we walked. "I am sorry to be poor company."

"Don't be sorry," I said. "I want to hear your story."

She looked at me long and hard, hard enough that I started to worry. Finally, she said, "It is awesome to work with you, Nellie Monroe."

Mary saw us smiling, but she didn't say a word.

16

Come-to-Jesus

Nona hugged me around the waist as we shuffled toward the clubhouse door.

"I love summer storms," she said, the stripes of our umbrella splashing movement and color onto her body and face. "Such drama and romance, I expect Bogart and Hepburn to come dancing through the puddles at any second."

I opened the door while she held the umbrella.

"Plus," she said, "storms make even dirt smell good."

I inhaled deeply as we entered, the heady fragrance of wet earth mingling with the bittersweet smell of fresh coffee.

"Nellie!" Tank roared from behind the counter. He snapped to attention, pulling his feet off their perch on the glass top. "What on earth are you doing? Bringing the most beautiful woman in TOWN to my shabby spot during a THUNDERSTORM?" He walked toward us, mitts outstretched. "Leila Byrne, YOU are a sight for this man's eyes."

"Tank," Nona said, "*you* are a hopeless charmer, but the trouble is, I see through it." Her eyes sparkled. "Have you talked with Mr. Winthrop lately?"

"Oh, come ON, Mrs. B.!" Tank groaned. "I'm a GROWN MAN. And that was forty years ago."

"I'm sure he'd appreciate knowing who stole the plastic cow outside his Dairy Sweet." She leaned against the counter, arms crossed and eyes twinkling. "What about Suzette Martins? I know she's not the school nurse anymore but—"

"Good luck," I said and patted Tank's shoulder on my way to the back of the clubhouse. Tank and Nona had a running dialogue on the merits of confession and as far as I knew, Tank had never come out ahead. Nona had seen him through a long and fruitful delinquency and had persisted in loving him when even his own mother stopped taking his calls. As a result, Tank had an undying affection for Nona, even when she brought to mind the endless list of wrongs he probably should make right. He crumbled every time. Inevitably, in the next week, I would see him in town with his ball cap curled in his beefy hands, looking a lot like a repentant Eddie Haskell.

I stood on tiptoes in the back room, rummaging through a stack of shelved papers in search of my check. Tank had called early that morning to relieve me of my scheduled hours because of the storm, but Nona had been in a funk and I knew we both needed a diversion. Nothing spelled diversion quite so well as a man named after military machinery.

The front door squeaked open, and I peeked out to take a look. Amos stood on the mat, shaking his head back and forth like a dog. Water sprayed out in either direction until Tank hooted.

"You keep that up and you'll have to go back home for more of that GLOP you put in it!"

Amos scowled but softened when he saw Nona. "Hello," he said, wiping his hand on his shirt before offering it to her. "I am Amos."

"Amos, it's lovely to meet you. I'm Leila, Nellie's grandmother." Nona reached to take his hand. "Pay no attention to this surly old man. He's merely jealous of your full head of hair."

One side of Amos's mouth lifted in a shy smile. "Thank you," he said. "You talk much nicer than Nellie."

"I heard that," I called from the back. In a moment, Amos joined me.

"It is the truth." He crossed his arms, daring me to disagree. "Sometimes it is the truth that injures the most."

"That's deep," I said. I was at the bottom of a stack of envelopes, one of several stacks peppering the room. Tank the visionary was not to be bothered with details like cleanliness and prompt salary checks. Koi ponds, mini-golf, charming elderly women, yes. File cabinets, no.

"Here!" I said, rump in the air, head near the floor, but victorious. "I have yours too." I straightened. "Payday," I said and handed him his envelope.

He took it with a scowl. "This does not matter," he said, lifting the check to eye level. "Without a woman to love a man, the money is not of importance. And you cannot buy me love."

So we'd moved to the Beatles. "I talked with Katie."

His eyes grew big. They were a darker blue than Katie's and flecked with green. "What did she say to you? Does she love him?"

I shook my head. "Pretty sure she loves you, champ." I sat on a stool next to the broom hooks and gestured for Amos to take the folding chair. "She didn't say a word about Yoder."

"You are not lying to my face?" He sat but just barely. His posture was extremely good, so much so that Misty Warren would have called him a fruitcake in junior high. "Why do you say she loves me and you know I should be glad?"

I tapped my head. "So many reasons. First and foremost, I'm a very smart girl. Ask anyone. Second, I'm a woman, and women know about love." I didn't recount for him my complete lack of personal experience in this area. Sometimes the client-investigator relationship allows for discretion. "Third, when I asked her about boys, she talked about you and only you. And she got teary."

He bit his lower lip and leaned back in the chair. Both hands behind his head, he balanced on the chair's back legs. "She still loves me. It is a difficult idea to hold in one's mind."

I watched him brood for a moment. "Amos. You look completely depressed. I thought you'd be happy."

He let the chair drop. "Of course I am the happiest. My wildest dreams are coming true. But it is not easy, this dream. Our love is a long and winding road."

"NELLIE!" Tank called from the front.

"Listen," I said, standing. "Just take it one step at a time. Let it be, all right? All you need is love, but I'm a mere walrus." Dang! I was on a roll!

"Nellie?" Tank came to stand in the back-room doorway. He looked shaken. "I think you should come."

I stepped around him and hurried to Nona. Her eyes were dark and shifty.

"Hi, Nona," I said. "Sorry I took so long. Should we go home?"

She looked at me, puzzled, but nodded. "We should go home, Annette."

My heart stopped in my chest. This was new. "I'm Nellie," I said, too loudly. "Nellie, your granddaughter."

Tank wrapped his arm around Nona, touching my shoulder with his fingertips. "I'll help you two to the car. It's quite the rainstorm, isn't it?" He spoke with such gentleness, I could feel my racing heart crack and bleed within me.

We walked slowly to the front door. I sensed Amos watching us, and I wanted to tell him again to be patient. Sometimes love was harder than it looked.

I was sitting on her bed that night when she said the words.

"Nellie, I'm going to die." And she took a sip of tea, as if she'd told me Biz keeps colors bright, wash after wash.

"Well, yes, I'd assume so," I said, but my voice had a tremor. "I will, too, so touché."

She didn't smile. "You need to think about me dying. So it won't hit you so hard when it happens."

I looked at her full in the face. "I've thought about it."

"Not much, you haven't. And the way you looked on the way home from Tank's tells me you're not one bit ready for it."

"So what am I supposed to do?" I said in my *High School Musical* voice. "Think macabre thoughts? Wear black? Imagine you in a casket?" That last one made my breath catch. I stopped.

"Sweetheart, I don't really like the idea of leaving you either. Solomon wrote that God sets eternity in the hearts of men. We're not wired to want to die or to watch the people we love leave us."

I was quiet. The quilt on Nona's bed was a patchwork of pinwheels, the scraps of fabric melting together in riotous bursts of color. I ran my fingers along the stitching, feeling the softness earned through years of human warmth and contact.

Nona put her hand over mine. "Time to look at me."

I raised my eyes to meet her blurred image.

"Nellie Augusta Lourdes Monroe, I love you."

"Nona—"

"Don't interrupt. It's rude, and I'm losing it, so you'd better let me talk while I'm thinking straight." Her smile made me ache all over. "I love you, and God has created you to be magnificent. I'm not sure what that will look like yet, but you might as well be patient. He's not finished until he's finished, a moment which happens to coincide with your dying breath."

"Sheesh, a lot of death chatter, Nona," I said. Tears ran down my face, and she brushed one away.

"Do you know how much he loves you?" She was staring straight through my eyeballs, but all I could feel was warmth, cashmere-like, spreading through me.

I didn't speak. For all my word-of-the-day calendars over the years, not one of them helped me in that moment.

She smiled suddenly, a full-blown, Christmas-morning grin. "Well, aren't *you* in for a ride."

"What?" I said. "What ride? Where? What does that mean?"

She laughed. "I have no earthly idea. But I can't wait to hear about it."

"Nona, I appreciate the God-and-his-indecipherable-mysteries thing, but I'm more of a typed-agenda kind of girl, okay? I'm not sure how this works, if you have some direct line or if Jesus dabbles in the psychic network...."

Nona rolled her eyes. "Nellie, don't insult him."

"Okay, well, I'm just saying I'd like to know what you know."

She yawned, her little jaw dropping all the way to her chest, her nose wrinkling with the force of her weariness. "I've already told you all I know. He loves you, he has bottomless reserves of forgiveness, and he'll pursue you to the end, even when you're a pill and long after I'm gone. Now," she said, bumping my tush with her knees, "get off my bed and let the old woman rest. It was a long day." She closed her eyes. "Would you mind turning out the light, dear?"

I watched her, listened to her breathing become regular, then conclusive, like the periods at the ends of sentences. Even after I turned out the bedside lamp, I watched her in the stubborn daylight of a summer evening. It left slowly, the light, in increments so subtle they made a girl think maybe it was as dark as it was going to get. But then, a quarter shade darker, and another, until not a sliver was left and I had to feel my way toward the door.

17

Forget and Forgive

I stretched my legs on the Adirondack chair. Matt sat in a twin chair beside me, watching with me as the sun hung on above the tree line. After a tedious day of inventory at the course and the perpetual need to shoo Tank out of my work, I was ready to be worthless.

"Rockin' sundaes," Matt said. He flexed his feet and sprawled, hands propping up his tangle of hair. "I've never had homemade caramel sauce, and I can see now what a shame that is."

"You're welcome." I closed my eyes against the brightness of the sun. Overhead ceiling fans mounted on the beadboard above us cooled an otherwise sultry part of the day. The back portion of our wraparound porch caught breezes from three directions, often making it the coolest part of the house on a summer's night. Pop and Annette had long ago installed three Humvee-sized AC units to accommodate our home's square footage, but once a hundred-year-old house, always one. My favorite coping mechanism remained ice cream and ceiling fans on the back porch.

I turned my head to one side, letting the sun's rays warm my left cheek. Squinting at him, I said, "I like your new glasses."

He took them off and looked at them, as if evaluating them for the first time. Slender frames, black with squarish lenses. I thought they complemented Matt in both personality and his wiry body. "You really like them?" he asked. "You don't think they're too passive-aggressive?"

"Passive-aggressive glasses? What, you mean they like you, then they hate you? They get up in your face and then retreat with compliments?" I turned my face back to the sun. "How many more years until you're licensed in this drivel so you can charge people giant sums of money to sort them out?"

He sighed. "Many years. Tens of thousands of dollars worth of years." Glasses back on, he said, "I'm glad you like them." He cleared his throat. "Nellie," he said. "I'm going to ask you a question, but I don't want you to freak out."

"Mmm," I said. Was there anything better than the pink your nose and cheeks earned in the last hour of the day? A last-chance sunburn.

"Was that a yes, you will try not to freak out, or a no, you have to freak out, it's your inalienable right?"

"When do I freak out, Matt? I'm probably the most calm, even-tempered person you know."

"Except for the time you threw your desk chair out the window of your bedroom because you got a B-minus in American Literature."

"I was robbed. Mr. Barrows hated me."

"And the time you walked up and down the street with a megaphone, shouting, 'Scum! Scum! The baseball season's done!'"

"They should have let us use the field for the used book sale."

"And the city council paint-gun incident."

I sighed. "Anomalies, all of them."

"Of course."

I turned back to face him, the chair's painted wood warm against my cheek. "Speak freely and without fear of freak-out."

"Right." He cleared his throat. "Nellie—"

"Wait." I held up my hand, listening. "Mrs. H. is here."

Matt scanned the porch, watching at the door behind us. "I don't hear a thing."

"Oh, she's coming all right. I didn't spend my entire adolescence listening for those rubber soles for nothing." And sure enough, the screen door banged to attention, and Mrs. H. came to stand a safe distance from Matt.

"I thought you'd gone home for the night, Mrs. H. And yet it is lovely, as always to see you." I smiled and nodded toward Matt. "You remember That Friend of Mine."

"Hello," Matt said cheerily. "Good to see you again. How's the grudge?"

Mrs. H. pursed her lips. "In the interest of moving forward, I'm going to ignore that comment."

Matt's eyebrows arched. "Well done. All the signs of a healthy resolution." He tilted his head slightly and peered through his new glasses. "Mrs. H., how does this make you feel?"

She sniffed. "I feel fine, which is just about the same as I've felt my whole darn life. Now." She withdrew an envelope from the pocket of her skirt. "If you wouldn't mind, take this to … ehm. Your father." She shook the paper in front of Matt's face, as if it were burning her fingers.

He grasped it but kept it aloft. "You wrote my dad a note?" He stared at the paper, not moving.

"And you'd better believe it's for his eyes only," she snapped. Then, more gently. "I'd appreciate your help." She looked like she was about to get sick.

Matt tucked the note carefully into a pocket on his cargo shorts. "My pleasure." He nodded at Mrs. H., and I could see kindness spill from his face. "This is good."

She took two slow but shallow breaths, then nodded quickly. She turned to go.

"Good night," I called. "I'd tell you to sleep well, but I'll bet you already will."

She lifted a hand without turning around.

Matt stared at the door. "What the heck was that all about?"

I leaned back again on my chair, taking my empty parfait glass with me. After a few furtive slurps of melted ice cream, I set it down on the table between us. "I think, dear Matt, we have just witnessed the miracle of forgiveness. Or at least a baby step in that direction."

"Wait a minute." He pushed me over to the side to make room for his rear on my chair. "Are you saying you knew about this? That she finally told you what happened?" He was leaning over me, and I noticed how defined his jaw had gotten over the summer.

"Have you lost weight?" I sat up on one elbow and checked out his face. "Your face looks like the face of a grown man. When did it get that way?"

He rolled his eyes. "I believe the process began at around age fourteen. You see, Nellie, boys and girls are different. Perhaps the best way to begin this discussion is to talk about something called—"

"I do not want to talk about any of your things or my things, thank you." I kept staring. "You have a jaw. It's a man jaw. And you have no zits and new glasses and you're tan." I put both hands on his shoulders. "Matt, I think you might be hot."

He blushed two shades of red. "Thanks." His voice was so soft I barely heard him, so I punched his arm to bring him back.

"Seriously. Good work." I lay back down and stretched my legs off the side of the chair. "And yes, I knew about Mrs. H. Your dad stood her up for their junior prom, and she's been mad about it for a million years."

"Ooh, that's rough. Though I can't imagine her being the life of the party."

I scowled. "Hardly the point. It was rude and insensitive and only a ploy to get Francine Waterson to laugh." I shook my head. "I'll bet she had the most annoying, tinny little laugh. And a pathetic vocabulary."

Matt stared at me. "I don't understand any of the words coming out of your mouth."

"Just know," I said, patting him on the head, "that I have encouraged our dear Mrs. H. to respond to your dad's friendly gestures and get on with her life. Apparently it's working. Maybe I should look into psychiatry. I seem to be *really* good at it." I gathered the two parfait glasses and stood. "I'm getting another sundae. You want one?"

When I reached the door, I looked back for Matt's response. He was sitting with his head in his hands. "Sure," he said, his voice muffled.

"I thought you'd be happy about Mrs. H.," I yelled through the door. He mumbled a response, but I couldn't hear the exact words. "And what were you going to tell me?"

He waited until I was back on the porch, handing him a fresh injection of sugar and cold. He pushed back in his chair, legs unfolding, and shook his head. "Nothing. I can't even remember." He licked a drop of caramel off his thumb.

I raised my spoon for a toast. "To new beginnings," I said. "Cheers."

He nodded and tipped his spoon into mine. "Exactly," he said, holding his glass still in front of him. He seemed to be somewhere else, and I allowed the silence, content to hear the breeze whistle its low-pitched approval of day's end.

18
Roll with It

I had my fist poised on the wood frame of the door, ready to knock, but I stopped to watch first. Grandma Mary sat with four young children at one end of the long kitchen table. They faced the door, Granny holding the hands of the two closest to her and swaying as they sang a peppy song in German. Two girls and two boys, all clearly from the same gene pool with their blond curls and bright eyes. The girls were dressed in dark purple with black aprons tied on the front. Their bonnets were the same style as the women's, only smaller and a bit tousled-looking. The boys had hats too, theirs brimmed and made of straw. The dark blue of their shirts played off the color of their eyes.

Granny Mary patted each one on his or her knee in time to the music, joining in on the last stanza. Her thin vibrato merged with the pure, unadorned voices of the children, and she closed her eyes as they finished.

She issued a percussive command in Pennsylvania Dutch, which I took to mean, "Get thy hineys back to work," or perhaps,

"Singalong with Grumpy Pants is over!" because they hopped off the table bench and ran giggling to the door. I opened it for them, catching a few curious glances before they headed to the wooden swing set out back.

"Come in," called Sarah, stopping her work of sweeping under the table. Elizabeth and Katie greeted me from the sink. Elizabeth stood by the hand pump and was letting water cascade into the tub of the sink, where it met with a mountain of dishes waiting to be baptized. Katie waved at me with a white dish towel.

"Wie Geht's?" I dropped it like a hammer, thanks to a late-night YouTube tutorial the evening before.

Elizabeth giggled, but Granny Mary tipped her chin at me in understated praise. "*Gut, danki*. I hope you are ready to be working, Nellie Monroe. No more chopping onions for you."

I caught Katie's eye, and she lifted her shoulders in a small shrug. Secretly, I just hoped we wouldn't have to butcher anything. I'd seen a group of men hanging out by what Katie had called the smokehouse. When they'd opened the door, I'd seen sinewy slabs of animal parts hanging from the rafters. I knew the meat I ate came from a living being, but I felt really good about it taking a detour onto a Styrofoam package before I took it home and fried it up in a pan. I thought of the bristly little hairs I'd seen on that piglet the last visit and gulped. "What are we doing today, Grandmother Mary?"

She let a bag of flour drop onto the counter. "Pastry crust. Wash all of your hands."

"Pastry?" Oh, that was not much better than hairy pigs. I did not flourish with pastry. In fact, I'd tried exactly two piecrusts in my life. One ended in a gloppy, Play-Doh mess and was inedible even to Gucci, our dog at the time. The other provoked weeping and indelicate language before it even got to the oven. Elizabeth pumped a fresh stream of water for me and pointed to a slab of brown soap. "Holy moly, did you make this?" I held up the bar and smelled it. Lavender.

"My mother did," Elizabeth said, leaning into her work of scrubbing a soiled pot. "We help, but she does the best job at the making of soap. She also makes honey oatmeal, lemon mint, and almond with orange." She lowered her voice. "Do not ask about this to Grandmother Mary. She prefers to use only lye soap."

I raised my eyebrows. "With pumice?"

Elizabeth giggled. "I know this pumice. It is just like Grandmother Mary. This is a good joke."

"Girls! Enough chatter. Nellie Monroe, it is the hour for pastry."

I dried my hands on a clean towel embroidered with flowers. "Grandmother Mary, isn't pastry awfully advanced? What about cookies? Or brownies? Or a cake? I love chocolate cake, don't you?"

Mary sighed. "You are talking always too much. So many words from one small body. Come."

The last word issued a command, and I scooted over to where she stood by the large table. She handed me a starched apron and waited while I tied the strings. She shuffled to the end of the table, muttering in Pennsylvania Dutch under her breath. After a quick tug on the bottom drawer, she straightened and waved a blue kerchief at me. "Take off that *kapp*. It is as large as a chicken. You must be able to see to make a good piecrust."

I nodded and untied my bonnet from my chin. It was all I could do not to moan with pleasure, a noise I was certain would not endear me to Granny. The kerchief weighed nothing in comparison to my bonnet. I tucked a stray curl into my ponytail holder and smiled hopefully. "Better?"

"You have so very much hair," she said. It was the closest she'd come to sounding impressed with me.

"Thank you," I said.

She sniffed, brought back to her usual disdain for all those imperfect humans around her. "Too much of anything is a sin," she said.

I was sinning because I had thick hair?

She added, "'Charm is fleeting, and beauty deceptive; but a woman who fears the Lord is to be praised.'"

I tried connecting my Nona to these words, clearly from the Bible she and Granny Mary both read. Perhaps because Granny's voice sounded so much like machine-gun fire, it was too distracting by the time she got to that part about praising.

She slapped a whisk into my hand and dumped the dry ingredients into a commercial-sized metal mixing bowl. "Flour, salt, sugar. Mix."

I whisked like I'd never whisked before. She was standing so close to me, I could count her individual breaths. When she was satisfied, she pointed to two packages wrapped in wax paper.

"To make a crust that flakes, you must use both lard and butter." She handed me a small knife. "Cut into pieces and combine with dry elements."

I reached for the butter but she karate-chopped my forearm. "Wait!"

I pulled my arm back from the fire of Sensei Mary. "What? Wait for what?"

"Wait to be ready." She narrowed her eyes at me. "Pastry has no patience. You begin only when you are ready. If you work the dough for too long, you will *ruin* it." She nodded.

I was staring at her eyeballs, watching her blink but not move her gaze from mine. "Well, that just makes me scared."

"Ah," she said. A smile began a pioneering expedition around her mouth. "And so there *is* humility in that head of large hair. This is good." She slapped the island with both hands. "You are ready."

I reached for the butter slowly. She was puny, but that karate chop had stung. When I'd set both slabs in front of me, I took a deep breath.

"This is not to be nervous," she said, pushing away that thought with one bony hand. "These will only be three pies, just enough for dessert tonight for our family. I give you a small job to start."

"Thanks," I said, incorporating the butter and lard into the flour mixture. Lard, as it happened, smelled exactly how it should with a name like that. It smelled piggy and fatty and like something one should never, ever touch without latex gloves.

"Hurry!" Granny Mary was breathing onto my shoulder. I could feel perspiration forming on my upper lip. "The dough will get tired. Here—add cold water."

"How much?" My voice was too high on the scale, but I was sweating over lard and flour. I couldn't be bothered with social niceties.

"How much water," she said, "is to depend on the weather, the humidity, the feel of the dough. You need more."

I emptied a tablespoon, then another, then another, until Granny grabbed the spoon out of my hand.

"Make into ball and we roll."

I took the long wooden rolling pin she offered and put it down gingerly on the ball of dough.

"You work it! Like this." Granny Mary pantomimed the rolling motion over her spot at the counter. I looked around to see if the other women were watching, but only Katie caught my eye. I could see she was very close to the Church Laugh, the one that cannot be unleashed without punishment and so becomes a girl's only thought and focal point. I myself had experienced this phenomenon on many occasions, and I did not envy Katie. One burst of laughter while Granny Mary was "working it," and she'd probably have to donate her body for the next batch of lye soap.

"There." Granny stood back, little dots of sweat beading her forehead. "Do not delay. Roll it now, Nellie Monroe!"

I rolled it, friend. Oh, did I roll it. I pushed and pulled and grunted and floured until Granny Mary grabbed the pin from me and pointed to three greased and waiting glass pie dishes.

"We will do one-crust pies today. Lattice top later." She took a thin spatula and loosened one crust from the counter. In one quick motion, she rolled the crust around the rolling pin and slipped it perfectly into one of the dishes.

I sighed. "The last time I tried this part, my crust looked like it had already been chewed."

Mary wrinkled her nose. "This is an unsavory image for the thoughts. Try it now before the dough becomes too warm."

My first attempt had the already-chewed problem and Mary *tsk*ed with disapproval. I clenched my jaw and floured the pin again. The second was a step up, at least to the competency of a four-year-old.

The final looked like Mary's if she'd been drinking, and I was sure she hadn't.

"*Gut*," she said. "We flute." She showed me how to push one knuckle between two fingers to make the fancy ripple effect on the top of the crust. A few fork pokes for venting, and we stepped back to admire our work.

"Nellie Monroe," she said finally, her eyes on the dishes, "do not become any more arrogant than you already are, but these are good piecrusts. I will eat a slice myself."

Sarah sighed happily or with relief, I wasn't sure which. Elizabeth and Katie smiled at me with encouragement.

"Thank you, Grandmother Mary. You helped me face my fear."

She sniffed. "Who fears a pie crust?" But I saw her smile as she lowered herself on a chair to rest.

We took our plates and glasses to a long picnic table that stood sentry under a weeping willow. Mary sat first, and we followed. The kitchen needed a breather after the baking, and we did as well. I patted my forehead with the edge of my apron and smiled at my piece of pie.

The three crusts had been filled with fruits of the Schrock garden. One raspberry, one rhubarb, one blueberry, all bursting with color and the promise of a really good snack. Sarah's face had shown surprise when Granny Mary had suggested we each take a plate out to the table off the front porch.

"It is appropriate," she'd said when Sarah had stared. "Nellie

Monroe should taste her first piecrust, and also this kitchen is too hot for work."

Katie had whispered to me as we plated five slices. "This I cannot believe! We work in the hot, the cold that freezes, the rain. Never do we stop for a piece of pie." She nudged me gently with her elbow. "Nellie Monroe has worked a miracle."

The breeze was cool under the beckoning fingers of the willow. I watched the languid branches brush each other, ask for a dance but then snap back in fidelity to their own stems. My slice of pie, from the raspberry, tasted just like it should, having been raised from birth by the hands of these hardworking women. I could smell the butter, the berries, vanilla, and a tidge of lemon, as I brought it to my mouth. The crust melted against my tongue, just the right mix of flaking and soft, sweet and salty. I closed my eyes and must have moaned my appreciation, because the girls giggled.

"Nellie, it is possible you have found your choice of work. Your profession," Elizabeth said. She pointed her spoon at me, recently cleaned from a helping of blueberry. "You enjoy the eating so much, and the crust is very good. You should be a cook."

I took a tarrying sip of lemonade, buying time. "I'm not too sure about that," I said, finally. *I'd rather spy on families like yours and bring secret information back to the people who hire me. Hey, anybody hear from Amos Shetler these days?* That answer didn't sound quite as diplomatic. I felt a tiny drop in my stomach. *It's not deceit,* I told the drop. *It's a job.*

The women had been chatting with enthusiasm as we ate, but suddenly the group fell silent. I looked up from my forkful of crust and juice and saw a man approach through the willow branches. He was roughly my age, but unlike most of the men I'd seen around the Schrock farm, he was beardless. This was fortunate because it allowed a perfect view of a movie-star smile.

I saw Katie's posture straighten and her jaw set.

"Who is that?" I whispered to Elizabeth, who held her glass of lemonade midair beside me.

"John Yoder," she said. "He will marry Katie this fall."

I spoke around a large bite of pie. "What?"

He parted the willow branches with one hand. "*Guten Owed*," he said, nodding at Granny Mary and Sarah. "Good evening," he said to Elizabeth and me.

"This is Nellie," Elizabeth blurted. "She is English, and she made the piecrust."

"I see," John said. He turned his full-wattage smile on me. "Hello, Nellie the English." Then his eyes searched Katie's. "*Guten Owed*, Kate."

She nodded. "Hello, John. How are you today?"

"I am well, thank you. You look to be well."

Elizabeth sighed softly beside me.

Sarah rose. "Would you like a piece of pie, John? Lemonade?"

He watched Katie, who exhibited a sudden interest in her fork. After a moment, he answered, a bit loudly. "Thank you, Mrs. Schrock. I am grateful for your kindness, but I must head back to my father's fields. I stopped to see your husband, and he allowed me to borrow a tool we need." He stepped toward Katie and placed one hand on hers. She lifted her eyes to his. "It is good to see you all," he said, and the other women murmured the same back to him. I said nothing because he sure-as-shooting wasn't talking to me.

When he'd walked out of earshot, Sarah and Elizabeth began a giddy discussion of what a lovely couple they made. They decided Katie would have eight children, that their engagement and wedding would be the first announced at church at the end of the summer, and that Katie would make a beautiful bride in deep indigo. Mary sat with a shrewd eye trained on Katie but said nothing.

I lingered with Katie as we cleared our dishes to go back inside. She fell into step behind the others, and I joined her.

"John seems like a nice man," I ventured. Actually, he'd seemed like the perfect front man for a boy band, but I didn't think Katie would grab onto that reference.

"Yes, he is," she said slowly. "He is a nice man, and he will be a good husband."

I couldn't shake the feeling that she was giving a book report instead of a summary of her fiancé's best traits. We climbed the wooden stairs to the porch and I couldn't take it. "Do you love him?" I mean, honestly. Who *was* I? Mr. Sandman? But there it was and she turned to me with a quick answer.

"No. I do not." She lifted her chin slightly, her eyes searching mine. "But my mother did not love my father either at the beginning. Sometimes love comes with years instead of minutes." She opened the screen door but let it shut without going inside. Handing me her plate, she said, "Nellie, will you tell the Schrocks I needed to go home? A headache. I have a headache."

I nodded, knowing a liar when I saw one but familiar with the headache ruse myself. I'd gotten out of an entire quarter of gym class because of a recurrent "headache."

"Thank you," Katie said, her smile warm and forgiving of my

P.E. lies, even though she couldn't have known. "You are a good friend. And," she drew out the word, "you are a good cook. Very good crust."

I held out my hand for her to slap five. "Thanks."

She slapped hard. "I will see you next week."

I watched her walk down the driveway at a clip, looking up every few paces but for the most part focusing only on the little bit of road in front of her.

19

Keep It Together

The thing about standing on your head is that it's an immediate jump start to perspective. Some people like going for a run. Matt was into that. He said the open road combined with the sounds of his breath and his ASICS hitting the pavement cleared his head of all the extras. I, on the other hand, preferred not to sweat. It was one thing if the sun was super hot and you were at the state fair. That was sweating with purpose. Pork-chop-on-a-stick purpose. But *making* myself sweat? Intentionally? That seemed like *trying* to fall out of a tree or *asking* to be frisked by airport security. No, thanks.

So running was out, as was most exercise other than an occasional punching bag. I didn't really get into talk therapy, though Matt had told me many times how much I needed it. Wiling away one's life at Wellman's Pub was certainly the most popular way of shifting perspective around Casper, but I didn't see how being sloshed would help my thought processes, as they were pretty amazing already. Plus, that was so cliché: Town Luminary Caves to Mediocrity and Loneliness and Drinks Herself to Oblivion. Very chic-tragic, but not for me.

Headstands were the ticket. All that blood flowing in a weird direction, gravity pulling your body mass toward the ground, coming very close to seeing stars and then letting go and crashing to the floor. It was fantastic. And I had some mind clearing to do. A paradigm shift was in the works for this case, and I needed to figure out how to tackle it. Amos loved Katie. Katie loved Amos. John loved Katie and was months away from marrying her and starting work on that beard. It appeared Katie was on board but kind of like a fish being on board to try out a hook. What had she said? Sometimes love came from years? A good-buddy marriage! Just how all great romances began! I needed to help this girl, and a good long headstand was the first step.

I was nearing the seeing-stars part when a knock sounded at my door.

"Come in," I said, though it sounded kind of warbled. My cheeks became a speech impediment when they hung upside down.

My parents entered en masse, which, for most of my life, had been a foreboding sign. They'd arrived on the late flight the night before, bronzed and smiley after two weeks in Banff.

"Pumpkin, eh, what's with the headstands?" My dad's boat shoes interrupted my line of sight. I glimpsed my mother's open-toed heels picking their way through the clothes that littered the floor.

"You'd love it, Pop. I can show you how, if you want." Because of the heavy cheek issue, my words sounded like I *had* been tipping a few back at Wellman's. "You might want to move."

"What's that?" Pop crouched down and then tilted his head upside down. "What did you say?" He enunciated like he did every time we went to France and he thought the cab driver simply needed more *consonants* in order to appreciate English.

"You. Move. Now. Please." The stars were obscuring a clear view of Pop's face, so I knew time was of the essence. He'd just cleared my trajectory when I let my legs timber down hard onto the carpet. I lay there, watching the ceiling turn back to its normal color.

Mother gasped. "Oh, my heavenly days."

I turned my head toward where she sat perched on my office chair. "Mother, people have been doing headstands—inversions, if you will—since the beginning of time. It's all over ancient historical record." This, I admit, was not something I'd verified with actual reading. It was more of a general feeling that I was probably correct.

"No, no, Nellie. I don't care if you stand on your head or on your earlobes, for that matter. I gave up understanding everything you do years ago. I'm talking about your hair. *Did you use a flatiron?*"

I pulled my fingers through the smooth strands, feeling a mix of kink with smooth. My technique was still spotty. "I sure did, Mother. And I hope you appreciate it." I sat up slowly. "I used to be able to get up and go. Stuff all that hair into a ponytail or under a ball cap and call it a day. Ironwork takes at least twenty minutes and that's after the hair's fully dried. Of course, it does last a few days, averaging the time to about ten minutes a day, which is more palatable."

She stared at me, wide-eyed. "Oh, honey, let's go shopping!" She clapped her hands and looked at Pop. "We can talk about this later."

He shook his head. "I don't think so, Annette. Shopping will wait."

She frowned. "I've waited nearly twenty-one years. I should think that would count for long enough."

"Nellie," my dad said. He cleared his throat. "Nellie," he said again.

"Oh, good gravy, Pop. If this is about the birds and the bees, I already know. Don't you guys remember in junior high when you had to sign the permission slips to watch *Girl, You'll Be a Woman Soon?"*

Pop looked ill. Mother swooped in to rescue. "Nellie, dear, we know you know about intercourse."

"Please never say that word in my presence again."

"All right," Pop said. His face was all red and blotchy. "Pumpkin, we need to talk about Nona. She's worse every time we see her."

"I think she's been really good the last few weeks. We debated nationalized health care a few days ago." I split my legs in front of me and stretched one hamstring. You wouldn't think it, but headstands can fatigue pretty much any muscle.

"She slept almost all of today, other than joining us for a very discombobulated lunch conversation." Annette sighed. "Your father is right, Nellie. We need to talk about the next step."

"You're not putting her in Fair Meadows." I shook my head once, hard. "I won't let you do that to her."

"Now, Nellie, we've known the Clausens for years, long before they owned Fair Meadows." Pop took on a measured tone. "I spoke with Bob this morning. They've just completed construction of a new facility on the west side. Have you been by there? Out by the McIntyre acreage?"

I said nothing.

"It's quite lovely from the outside," Annette said. "Beautiful stone work, all limestone brought in from that place in Minnesota. What was it, Clive? St. Croix?"

"I believe you're right," Pop said, nodding. "Just off the river on Highway—"

"Oh, stop," I said, hauling myself to my feet. "I will not be carting Nona off to the Shady Acres of Doom just so she can enjoy the indigenous limestone. Are you serious?" I stacked Amish research books on my desk. "Don't you know what happens to people who go there?"

Pop spoke. "They die."

"Clive, please," Mother said, watching my horrified face.

"It's true," Pop said, shrugging. "I don't mean to sound callous, but you two both know I'm right. Nona is going to die, and so are we." He rubbed his forehead with a hand and paused. "I'm just trying to figure out how to do the best we can for her."

Mother moved to sit by him on my bed. She put one skinny arm around his broad shoulders and looked at me. "Bob said that it's easier to make the transition when a patient is doing well than when she is not. They don't recommend waiting until it's a … a fight."

I shook my head and set my jaw. "No. My answer is no, and her answer will be no. She will hate it, and I will hate it more. I can take care of her here. Until the end."

"Nellie, you know she doesn't want that." Mother's voice was soft but strong.

"She's said so from the beginning," Pop said to the carpet, his head still in his hands. "Since the first and only doctor's appointment when she refused an aggressive workup. 'No lingering, no wrestling with the inevitable, and no way Nellie devotes her life to me like a nun.' Remember that speech?" He let a wry laugh escape.

"Well, we're not even close to the lingering part. And I'm not a nun." My insides trembled, and I thought I might be sick. They sat in my room and on my bed, but I was the one to leave. "No," I said one more time before hitting the hallway.

We were fine.

Amos met me at the mall. He'd said he wanted "the opinion of a female" as he was in the market for some new clothes. He didn't seem to notice that I wasn't exactly a good resource for this type of information; I had not yet parted with the denim purse. Still, I figured if I could broaden his palette outward from the fluorescent color grid, it was progress.

My feet felt heavy, the burden of my conversation with Mother and Pop reverberating hollow echoes in my gut. I rounded the corner on the upper level and glimpsed Amos before he saw me. Amos wasn't particularly tall, but he did stand out. He waited in front of Slash, hands in his pockets, making inappropriately long eye contact with the people who passed him. He was smiling, but it was a fixed smile. Someone must have told him that was how it worked in casual social settings. I sighed.

"Hi, Amos," I said when I approached. "Don't stare. Just look and move on. Like this." I did a quick eye-lock with a passing mother with young children. She smiled hopefully, and I looked away.

"You made her sad," he said, smiling extra long as she passed him.

"No," I said, all patience. "That's just how women with young children look. They look sad. That's no reason to creep them out."

A bouncy blonde girl approached us. "Hi! Welcome to Slash! Can I help you find anything?"

I sniffed. "Um, we're not even inside the store. Is that what your manager tells you to do, accost customers when they're still outside?"

The girl looked like she might cry. "Sorry. I'm sorry. It's my second day and—"

Amos cleared his throat. "Do not be apologizing. It is I that am sorry. This person"—he gestured to me like I smelled foul—"she is the cranky pants. Please forgive us." The whole time, he stared without blinking at Bouncy. Never moved his gaze, kept the creep-o smile on his face. And Bouncy *liked* it.

"You're very nice," she said, awfully shy for a person who'd just evangelized for a clothing store. "My name's Jordan." She put out her hand to shake.

He took it carefully. "Jordan. Just like the river," he said, awe in his voice.

She blushed, and I was certain she'd never heard of the Jordan River in her life.

He followed her into the bass-thumping music and bright lighting but threw a warning glance in my direction. "Do not be ill-tempered," he said.

I rolled my eyes. Honestly. He was the one who'd been living in cultural seclusion for his whole life, and he thought *I* was the one who needed pointers?

"Are you looking for anything special today? We're having a sale on all our graphic tees." She pointed to a display of shirts. "And our denim is thirty percent off when you open a Slash card. Do you have a Slash card?" This entire speech was of utmost seriousness to Jordan, who may or may not have known what a river was.

"I do not have any card," Amos said. He opened his billfold and produced a thick stack of bills. "I will pay with cash, thank you. I feel discomfort with creditors."

She nodded and tucked the money back into his wallet, closing it and pushing it gently toward him. "You're a smart guy," she whispered. "Just don't let anyone else see all that money, okay?" She smiled at Amos, and I frowned. It was uncomfortably difficult to be annoyed with someone who was nice to Amos. He was kind of like an animal rescue dog to me. I cut Bouncy some slack.

When she'd set Amos up in a dressing room with heaps of clothes, none of which looked like they'd walked off the set of *Miami Vice,* I thanked her.

"Oh, I'm happy to do it!" Her hair vibrated with sincerity. "You're welcome to stay back here with him. The common area is *totally* gender-neutral." She promised to check back on us in a few minutes then went to help a baffled-looking father and his teenaged daughter.

"This shirt has words on it." Amos's voice was muffled in the dressing room. "It says WORK IT LIKE YO MOMMA ISN'T WATCHING. What is the meaning of this?" He opened the door to the dressing room, dressed in a kelly green T-shirt with white block lettering. The jeans looked to bc about two sizes too small with cuffs that stopped at his anklebone. Bouncy hadn't conquered the Slash fitting chart just yet.

Amos stood in front of the three-way mirror. He smiled. "I like this denim."

I shook my head. "No, you don't. Next."

He looked confused. "Not the shirt either?"

"It means shake your tush in a way your mother wouldn't like."

He looked horrified and strode toward the dressing room, shutting the door with a bang. "Tell me," he called, "how was your visit yesterday to the farm of the Schrock family?"

I looked at my reflection in the three-way. *Here goes.* "I met John Yoder."

The door to the dressing room flew open, and Amos stood, one arm in a new T-shirt. He was painted into another pair of jeans, these pinstriped and, again, too short. "John Yoder. And is it true? Nellie?" He walked over to the bench where I sat and lowered himself next to me. I could see our reflection, half-dressed Amish Amos and me with my new hair and same old purse.

I turned and put both hands on his shoulders but then pulled back. "Um, can you put the shirt all the way on? It's a little awkward, skin on skin." I was sure the beauty parlor girls would be hyperventilating, but it just wasn't working for me.

"Yes, of course." He pulled his arm through the sleeve. The shirt was fire-engine red and had light blue lettering that read, I KNOW, I KNOW. IT'S HARD NOT TO STARE.

I sighed. "Amos, Katie and John are pretty much engaged. They'll announce it after the harvest and are getting married in October."

He looked at me so long, I feared he'd had some kind of medical incident, some sort of graphic-tee palsy. Finally, he blinked and said,

“Thank you, Nellie. I will pay you now for your work.” He stood and mumbled something about his wallet.

“Hi, guys!” Jordan was back, this time wearing a headset. “How are we doing for sizes?” She looked at Amos’s ankles. “Ooo, no. That’s not good. I’ll be back.” She said something into the headset and left without hearing a word from us.

“Wait, Amos,” I said, following him to the dressing room. “You can’t pay me yet. We’re not finished.”

He shook his head. “It was true. She is marrying the Slim Shady, John Yoder. I am helpless to change her mind. I am paying you now.” He picked up his wallet, but I pushed the money away.

“Amos, she doesn’t love him.” I forced him to look at me. “She looked as miserable as you do.”

He waited.

“We’re not finished with this. That girl isn’t going to marry someone she doesn’t even love. Not on my watch.” I caught a glimpse of my reflection, arms crossed, chin tilted in defiance to all things Yoder. *Very* impressive for someone with no experience in the dramatic arts.

He slammed down his wallet. It hit the concrete floor with a thud. “You are correct, Nellie Monroe, PI. We are not going to stop our fight to the death. Katie will be saved by her Moondoggie, or my name is not Amos Benjamin Shetler.”

“I thought you stopped watching *Gidget*.”

He shrugged. “It is such the good television program. Not like the trash on these days of the twenty-first century.”

Jordan returned with an armful of denim. “Hi, folks. These should work better.”

I waved. “I’m off. You kids have fun.”

Jordan balked. “Um, maybe you should stay. My boss says always to defer to the girlfriend.”

Amos and I snorted in sync. “She is not my girlfriend,” he said, shaking his head as he reentered his dressing room. “She is not the girlfriend of *anyone.* She punches men in the stomach.”

I sighed. “It happened once,” I said quietly to Jordan.

“Twice!” Amos called. “She is a most frightening girl.”

When I left, Amos and the Jordan River were weighing in on a pair of Bermudas and a matching pink shirt. “Frightening,” like most things, was completely relative.

20

Honestly

The next morning, I had the early shift at the golf course. This adjective, *early*, means many things to many people, but to Tank it meant be behind the counter not a minute after six.

"You got all winter to SLEEP," he'd say with a look of disgust. "You YOUNG people don't know that daylight in our NORTHERN CLIMATE is something to savor, something to CHERISH. Start 'er up at SIX BELLS and quit your whining!"

Fortunately, I was not averse to early mornings. Though not a chatty person at that hour, I was at least able to offer a pleasant countenance to the senior citizens who liked to golf just after sunrise.

"NELLIE!" Tank barked from the bathroom where he was dealing with a leaky faucet. Despite my repeated offers to call a plumber, he would have none of it. This was the fourth consecutive day spent on the drip with no resolution in sight.

"Yes, Tank?"

"How's your beautiful grandma? She back to her sweet SELF again?"

This was not a conversation best yelled. Nevertheless, Tank was a man who needed his space when emotions arose. I knew he was worried in his own head-under-the-sink way.

"She's doing better, Tank, thank you." I tore the cellophane off a package of balls destined for driving-range buckets. "She still knows you're full of malarkey, for one thing."

I heard him snort. "That woman would say NO SUCH thing about me, and you know it. She knows QUALITY when she sees it. She lived through the Depression, for Pete's sake."

The bell above the door announced another golfer. I looked up from the bucket of balls to see Matt blazing a trail for the counter.

"Matthew DuPage, what on earth are you doing out of bed at this hour?" I peered at his face. "You look horrible. What's wrong with you?"

He sighed. "Nellie, do you *have* an internal censor? Because the rest of us have a little flashing light that goes off in our brains when we think of saying 'you look horrible' to someone else. You don't have the censor, do you?" He pulled Tank's stepladder from behind the counter and opened it. He sat heavily, his hair falling into a tired face.

"But you look really bad. Aren't you sleeping?" I poured him a cup of coffee.

"Not really," he mumbled. He thanked me for the coffee and gulped his first swallow. "I've been, um, thinking too much."

"Just a sec. Eighteen, nineteen—" I was counting the bucket balls. Tank was a stickler when it came to making sure each bucket had fifty and not one more. This was no CHARITY, he was known to remind us.

Matt cleared his throat when he saw I'd finished. "I've been thinking. And I've been reading. I'm in a really worthwhile book right now called *Honesty: The Courageous Choice*."

I tore open another package of golf balls and looked at him. "That title makes me nauseous." I shook my head. "How can you plow through that stuff? Isn't it kind of common sense?"

"Well, yes. But no, not always. Sometimes it's really difficult to be honest. But look at what it's done for my dad and Mrs. H. They went to a movie last night." He smiled, and I smiled back, knowing the thrill of conquest. Plus, you can't not smile when Matt DuPage smiles at you. It's a rule of the universe.

"Do you think they make out?"

He stopped smiling. "That's gross."

"No, it's not. What? They can't kiss because they're old? Are you an ageist?"

"Pretty much, particularly when it has to do with my own father. Sick."

I waved my finger in his face. "You say that now, but you just remember that *you* will one day be an old people. And you'll still want to be kissed."

He blushed, and I noticed again how good-looking he was getting to be.

"I'm telling you, Matt," I said, "nice man-face. You're pretty cute." I reached over the counter to pinch his ruddy cheeks.

He batted me away, but I could tell it was a fake pout. "So, this book, about honesty. I've, um, been meaning to talk to you about some of the author's theses."

I widened my eyes. "You think I should be *more* honest? I thought I needed a filter."

Matt nodded as he took a gulp from his coffee cup. "Right. You do. But honesty in relationships can always improve. Even for people who, for example, punch people in the face or gut when trying to show affection."

I sniffed. "Who says that has anything to do with affection? Anyway, you sound like Amos."

"Amos?"

"Yes. He was just giving me grief about this same issue yesterday when we were shopping."

"Shopping."

"Haven't you noticed the predilection for DayGlo? It was time. A bit unnerving when he didn't have his shirt all the way on, but we made it. Did you know Slash has 'totally gender-neutral' dressing rooms? This comes from a trusted source, one wearing a headset."

Matt was staring out the side windows, sipping his coffee.

"Amos, now there's a person with an interesting take on relationships," I said. "I mean, here he is, all alone in the outside world. Well, not entirely alone. He has me, for one. But you understand what I'm saying. He's having to rethink everything he's ever taken for granted, from the way he spends money to what he wears to what it means when a girl flirts with him. You know?"

Matt said nothing.

"You're not listening," I said. "And you're very think-y. I can see why you aren't sleeping well. Too much thinking makes Matt a tired and nonresponsive conversation partner."

He turned away from the window and smiled sadly at me. "I'm listening." He pushed his empty coffee cup onto the countertop and stood. "Heard every word."

"I guess this is good-bye, then," I called after him as he walked out the door, hands in his pockets. "Weird," I said to myself.

"What's THAT?" Tank called.

"I said, 'WEIRD.' People are weird."

"Young lady," he said, "don't EVEN get me started."

I knocked on the attic door. "Popsicle delivery," I said, my voice loud to compete with the music blaring on the other side. "Nona, it's me, Nellie."

"Oh!" I heard her pad toward the door. She opened it wide and studied my face. "Can I help you?"

Okay. So today was a not-so-great one. They'd become more frequent, but I had not felt the need to tell Pop and Annette, who were gone again, this time in the Catskills for a tournament benefiting the Byrne Family Foundation. There was no need to alert them every time Nona couldn't remember my name. In the deep, important parts of her, she knew who I was, even if her brain wasn't cooperating. I'd simply roll with the not-so-good days.

"Hi." I smiled. "I'm Nellie. I brought some Popsicles for us to share."

"Oh, please, do come in."

Light filled the room, both from the arching windows and because Nona had every single lamp and overhead light switched on. I followed her to her canvas, which was covered in so much dark paint, it extended outward in a three-dimensional aesthetic. I handed her the lime Popsicle and kept the raspberry.

She held the wooden stick with paint-splashed fingers. "This is my absolute favorite kind," she said, delight on her face. We ate in silence, smiling at each other every other bite and murmuring our approval when we'd hit on a piece of frozen fruit.

"Nona, your new painting is very dark." I pointed with my Popsicle and watched her reaction.

She nodded slowly, letting a big bite melt a bit in her mouth. "Yes, it certainly is. You know, dear, life is not always easy. Sometimes it looks a lot like that." She turned away from the painting. "And sometimes it's sunny and bright and full of good treats and good friends." She nodded at me, the sunlight picking up gray and green flecks in her eyes.

"Absolutely," I agreed, trying my darnedest to not feel anything but just that moment. At any time, she would come back, sometimes even shaking her head as if to clear it from the rubble that had blocked her view. Other times, though, she stayed wherever she was, content to be there, unhurried and seemingly unconcerned about the length of her absence.

"Now, tell me what it is that you do. Do you own a dessert shop? Because this is exceptionally good. Compliments!" She tilted her head to bite around the stick.

"No, I'm a private investigator. In fact," I spoke slowly, mulling over how much I should say, "I'm working on an interesting case right now."

"You don't say?" Her eyebrows arched. "What a fascinating line of work." Her weathered hands, which had so many times gripped a paintbrush, held my own hands, cupped my face, folded into each other on her lap. She watched me expectantly. "I'd love to hear about it if you have a moment."

Oh, Nona. All I want anymore are more moments. "Well, there's this man named Amos." I told her about our playground hiring session, with a few embellishments involving a fedora and the rumble of distant thunder. Nona was a great listener. She gasped when I told her of my ruse with Professor Moss and how I'd gained entry to the Schrock home. She swooned over Amos's rivalry with John Yoder and his undying love for Katie. And she grimaced at the recounting of Grandmother Mary and her bone-crushing personality. By the time John was parting the willow branches during our pie break, Nona was flushed with emotion.

"Well, that girl has no business marrying a man she doesn't love." She got up from her chair and began to pace. "I should know. You cannot force a person to love you any more than you can force yourself. You can pretend very well." A bitter laugh escaped her throat. "I've known women who've pretended their whole married lives! But what does that get a girl?" She pointed at me from across the room before she made her way back, slender legs just working it out on the Berber carpeting. "It gets her a lifetime of heartache, that's what!" By the time she reached me, her eyes were back to the real Nona, feisty and alive.

"Nellie, sweetheart. I want to talk to you about Matt."

"Okay, Nona," I said, my heart full. She could talk to me about carburetors, for all I cared. It was just so good to see her.

"He is hopelessly in love, and you're not helping him one bit."

"Matt?" My eyes bugged. "In love? Oh, my gosh. That's why he looks so horrible. He can't sleep, he thinks too much, he stares out windows…." My stomach lurched. "Who is she? Did he say her name?"

My Nona, the pinnacle of patience, rolled her bright eyes. "Nellie, he loves *you* and has since you were children. Honestly, I thought you were the genius around here."

I stared at her lips, then my eyes darted to her eyes. She'd *seemed* so lucid, and yet she was speaking nonsense.

She shook her head and went to the little minifridge and freezer where I'd stashed the opened box of Popsicles. "I can see you want me to prove this." She sighed into the billows of frost escaping from the freezer. "Oh, lovely! My favorite kind!" She tore the wrapper off a cherry treat. "Let me see.... He watches you with moony eyes."

"He does no such thing. That's just the way Matt looks."

"It's normal to you because he developed this crush in junior high and you probably can't remember how he looked at you before that. Number two: He laughs at all your jokes."

"I'm funny."

"Not that funny, dear." She offered me a bite, but I shook my head. My insides were quivery enough as it was. "Number three: He told me."

I said nothing, just sat with my mouth agape. Looking back, I can't imagine that this pose, so often revisited during the following weeks, was an attractive one. It pretty much canceled out any progress made with my hair, but I couldn't help it. Nona was talking crazy when she wasn't crazy, and it had to do with Matt and me. In *that* way. The sky was falling, people.

"He told me years ago, Nellie, and he's kept his secret through all your friendship. Oh, I'm sure there were times when he convinced himself otherwise, when he told himself you weren't interested or that he wasn't interested. But I'm afraid he's always loved you, sweetheart. It's time you woman up and deal with it." She slapped her second clean Popsicle stick on the coffee table like a gauntlet.

"But—what—how—why—?" I could have thrown in a few more interrogatives while I was at it, so muddled was my thinking. "I don't understand how you knew all this time and he knew but I didn't know."

Nona leaned forward in her chair and fixed her gaze on me. "Nellie Augusta Lourdes Monroe, I love you more than anything on this planet. But that doesn't change the fact that you're the dumbest smart girl I've ever known."

I scowled and started to protest.

"Nope." She clapped one hand over my mouth. "I'm too old to hear your feeble argument. You're a luminary, I know, I know, but you are beloved by a sweet, sweet boy, and it's never even occurred to you." Her face softened. She stared at my face for a moment and then kissed me softly on the forehead. When she pulled away, her eyes were shining. "God is so good, isn't he?" She took in my face, smoothed my wrinkled brow with her fingers. "He knows just what we need and is so openhanded in his giving. He gave you to me, and"—she sighed—"he gave Matt to you."

"Nona, I'm kind of overwhelmed."

"Oh, I'm not saying you have to marry him, though you could do much worse. It just amazes me every time, and I've seen it over and over again, how God provides people for each other. Perfect fits, even with all our quirks and differences and crazy wiring." She sat back in her chair and closed her eyes.

I watched her, listening to her breathe, a small smile still on her face. When I got up, I tiptoed around her, taking care not to stir her from her sleep. I was almost to the door when I heard her speak, her voice cozy and tired but clear.

"I love you, sweet girl."

I knew that. I may have been the dumbest smart girl on the block, but to my very last cell, I knew that.

21

Uncharted Territory

Perhaps you're thinking, *Oh, good. She finally got it. Girl with the unfortunate hair finds true love and doesn't dillydally any longer in getting there.* Certainly the wisest course of action, looking back, but I'm afraid I dillied and I dallied. Instead of facing the whole thing head-on, I threw myself into good old-fashioned denial and procrastination. Matt didn't call for a full week, but when he did start up again, I'd let it ring and instead send him a cheery and impersonal text. For example:

Hey—Saw I missed your call. SWAMPED at work. Hope all is well with you!

Or:

Sorry I couldn't pick up. Hanging out with Nona a lot. See ya!

I mean, it shamed even me, using an elderly relative as an emotional shield. I'd just stare at the phone, his Michael Jackson ringtone playing "Man in the Mirror," and I'd freeze. There I was, a girl of twenty years, and I didn't know how to talk to a boy. That he was the boy who'd seen me in headgear, let me wear his ball cap when I'd undergone a very sketchy spiral perm, and taught me how to slow dance for my first homecoming—those details flew to the periphery when his number flashed on the screen. All I could think about was his new jaw and his sleeplessness, and I'd start chewing my nails, a habit I thought I'd kicked in seventh grade.

So rather than confronting my best friend with his unrequited love and facing what that might mean for me, I spent more time with the Amish. Naturally. There was nothing quite so escapist as hanging out in a boiling kitchen with turn-of-the-century technology to keep one's mind off one's romantic troubles.

"This corn pudding does not have a taste." Granny pulled a face. "Did you put in the salt?"

I nodded.

"Not enough." She put down her spoon. "It is so sweet, the children will eat it. But no man will, not in my home."

"Not in your administration," I said, just a little too snippy.

She narrowed her eyes at me, and I could feel Sarah staring over her potato ricer.

"Sorry," I mumbled. "That was over the line."

A small smile appeared, the visage of a victor. "You are one hundred of the percentage correct, Nellie Monroe. The English may not teach their children how to speak with respect to the elders, but the Amish do. I accept your apology." She pushed an empty dish toward me. "No more pudding today. Now we cut the cherries for crisp."

I left two hours later, my belly full of warm sweet crisp, and met Katie on the driveway. Seeing her caught me off guard, a feeling for which I immediately chastised myself. Katie was the reason I was even visiting the Schrocks, but lately I'd been more preoccupied with corn pudding and ignoring my best friend than solving my case.

"Pathetic, worthless, bad, bad PI!" I said under my breath. "Focus!"

"Hello, Nellie," she called out in greeting. The girl had great teeth, Crest commercial white, even and straight. The smile was killer, and I knew *she'd* never worn headgear, dirty rotten sucker.

"How are you?" I stopped near the weeping willow where John Yoder had visited. "You're later than usual."

She nodded and squinted into the sun, which fought on without mercy, even though it was after four in the afternoon. "I am late because my mother took measurements for my wedding dress."

"Wow," I said. "That's a big step."

She shook her head and glanced toward the road. "No, not very big. The Amish do not have large, fancy weddings like the English. I will wear a new dress, but it will be plain. Blue and simple and one that I will wear many times after the wedding."

I thought of my mother's bridal gown hanging enshrined in her closet. It was formidable, with yards of satin, lace, and rhinestones. She'd told me what it had cost, and that many dollars, even twenty-five years ago, would have gone a long way toward eradicating debt in the Gambia. Despite the significant investment, the dress had hung, lifeless and unworn, for its entire shelf life with the exception of Mother and Dad's first anniversary, when Annette had tried it on to make sure she hadn't gotten fat.

"Right. We English are more into buying shamefully priced dresses that poof out in ways we'd never normally permit and then putting them away in boxes, never to be worn again." I nodded at the simple lavender dress she was wearing. "It's probably a better idea to have the wedding be about the marriage instead of about the wedding."

She nodded. "That is what John says."

I waited while she scanned the empty road, seeming to look for someone or something that did not appear. After a moment, she blew a definitive puff of air toward her forehead, making the tendrils near her hairline quiver before falling again. She turned to me. "I hope you have a lovely evening, Nellie." She smiled and started to walk to the house.

"Wait." I turned, feeling a familiar churning in my gut. I'd had the churn many times throughout my life, usually resulting in faulty decision making on my part. I felt it just before I told Mrs. Wozinski that she'd be a better bank teller than English teacher. I felt it as I stepped onto the field for my debut and only performance as a twirler with the Casper High Marching Marvelettes. I felt it after I told the pastor of our church that I thought adult baptism was a great way to break up a rambling sermon if he needed a few moments to refocus. The churn started up as Katie turned back to me, her cheeks flushed with the heat and eyes bright with curiosity. That should have been my warning light to stop, drop, and roll right out of there without saying another word, other than a congenial good-bye or a "Try the cherry crisp. It's great!"

"Katie, what if I told you I could find Amos?"

She froze, the cornflower blue in her eyes as intense and prophetic as the wash of sky overhead. "Amos." She said the name as a declaration, a statement of irrevocable fact.

"Would you want to see him? Before you marry John and start trying to love him and—"

She cut me off with a hand outstretched. "Nellie, this is not possible. I know from my *rumspringa* that the world is large and it takes you in and …" She trailed off, her breathing shallow and quick. "Amos has been gone for months, and he knows where I live. If he wanted to speak to me, he could come to find me all by himself." The tremble in her voice betrayed a softness underneath the harsh words.

"I understand," I said, my tone careful. "If you change your mind, I think I can help. You know," I said, and she met my gaze, "if you think of it when you're fitting that new dress."

She stood with both fists clenched at her sides, her chest rising and falling in shallow breaths. When she spoke, it was just above a whisper. "He left."

I nodded slowly. "I know," I said.

She was still facing the road when I walked away.

I picked Amos up on the way home. He'd answered his cell before the first ring, which I hadn't known was possible.

"Hello, it-is-your-luckiest-day-this-is-Amos."

"Amos, that is borderline skanky."

"Hello, Nellie Monroe!" I could hear a rhythmic hammering sound in the background. "I am close to finish the hole number fourteen at the mini-golf. You are sure to think it is rocking your world. It has a windmill."

"I'll be there in ten minutes." I turned onto the highway leading to the golf course.

He hooted. "This is the best time of reaction! You are so fast to respond, Nellie! As when you punched me in the stomach!"

I rolled my eyes. "Be ready to go. We need to talk."

When we entered Margot's Coffee Nook a half hour later, it took me a moment to regroup. The smell of fresh grounds was an odd pairing with the frigid air pumping through the vents. I'd suggested something to cool the palate and the underarms, such as DQ or the freezer section of TasteWay. No chance, Amos had insisted. He'd "found out about the espresso." And there was no turning back.

We sat and were swallowed by two leather chairs placed by the fireplace, which, thank God in his mercy, was unlit. I took an indulgent sip of my iced water and assessed Amos over the lip of my glass. I saw him doing the same.

"What happened to your movie star hair?" he asked. "This is the old hair that is very large on your head."

I scrunched up my face in annoyance. "Ninety percent humidity does not allow for movie star hair." I tightened my ponytail for emphasis.

He shook his head. "This is not the truth. I have read in the *People* magazine that many movie stars with this curly hair find good ways to make straight their locks. The Sarah Jessica Parker, the Debra Messing, the Taylor Swift—"

"Taylor Swift curls her hair with a curling iron," I interrupted. "And all of those women have full-time stylists who have sworn off normal, healthy lives to devote themselves to making another person look good in airbrushed photos. A completely shallow existence."

"The Minnie Driver."

I gulped water and then pulled my bare arm across my lip. "As long as we're on the subject, what's up with *your* hair?"

He patted it gingerly and grinned. "It is this most excellent thing called Electrify Pomade."

I stared at his coif. The hair was clumped into product-heavy sprigs that shot heavenward. The clumping was not uniform, however; some of them thumb-width and others only a few hairs' worth. "Quite the technique."

He took a draw of his brewed Colombian with a double espresso depth charge. "I found Electrify Pomade at Target, a store that has every item a person can want. Perhaps you should look there for a styling aid for that curly hair."

"Thanks for the help," I said, my impatience lost on him. "Listen, Amos. We need to figure out our plan of attack."

His face grew serious, and he set his drink on the stone hearth. "I will not attack Katie. Men who attack women are nasty."

"I don't want you to attack Katie. I just mean we need to decide what we're doing next." I paused. "I told her I could set up a meeting between you two."

His eyes bugged. "This is very dangerous for her. She could get into very much trouble." He started bouncing his leg up and down, smacking a nearby table with each bounce. "I would fall downward in joy to see her again, but it is impossible. She was baptized. They would cut her off forever, like me." Bounce, bounce, hard bounce.

I reached over and slapped my hand down on his knee, which provoked one last attempt at a bounce. Keeping my hand in prevention position, I said, "You wanted to know if she loves John, and we found out she does not. But she's working on it, Amos, and she's a few weeks away from marrying him and having babies with him. Lots of little bonnet-wearing babies."

He shuddered. "With John Yoder."

"Exactly. So—" I stopped in midsentence, my hand on Amos's leg but my eyes stuck on Matt, who stood just behind him.

Amos turned to see the object of my open-mouthed staring. "Matt!" he called, waving with full arm movement, as if he were standing on the opposite end of a crowded football stadium. "Come on to sit down." He slapped the empty leather chair next to him. "We would like your advice."

Matt padded over, his eyes on Amos. "Hey, buddy," he said. Then a nod at me. "Hi, Nellie."

I watched his face, normally easy for me to read but today inscrutable. Friendly, pleasant even.

"How are you?" I didn't mean for it to be a loaded question, but all I could think of was my halfhearted texting. And his face, which had a deep tan and really nice lips, it turned out. I looked away before he answered.

"Great, thanks. Busy." He flopped down on the chair. "What's this about advice?"

Amos turned to face Matt. "It is a problem I have. With … you know." At this, he actually shoved Matt like they were dishing after prom. "The *women*. Heh, heh."

I tried not to vomit in my mouth, watching them both heh, heh. "There is a woman *present*, remember."

Matt cleared his throat. "Right, right. Sorry. So what's your woman trouble, Amos?" I felt Matt's eyes on me as I crunched an ice cube between my teeth. "I'll just tell you right now, they're a wily species."

"Yes!" Amos slapped Matt on the back. "Very wily! This woman, she is haunting to me, you know? I think about her, I dream about her, I wonder how she is …"

Matt raised one eyebrow, eyes on me. "You could just ask her."

Amos clapped once, loudly. "This is just what Nellie says! I should ask."

Matt waited until I looked up from my empty glass. "Nellie's usually right."

I bit my lower lip. *Except for when my oldest and best friend might have a crush on me and I can't speak because he's developed a stunning complexion,* I thought. *Except then. Then I'm really* not *right.*

Matt nudged me with his foot. "Hello? Anyone there? I haven't seen you this quiet since the day Doug Lambert lifted your skirt at recess in third grade."

Amos hooted. "This is a funny thought! Nellie in a skirt!"

I swallowed hard and looked at Matt. "I'm just listening. I'm trying to be a better listener."

Matt's face was screwed up in concentration. "You are." A statement, not a question, as if it were simply too difficult to believe.

"Yes," I said, nodding with all the earnestness within. "I have been a very, very bad listener for most of my life. I'm repenting."

"You're listening and repenting." He watched me for a moment, his face all confusion. "Well. That's very interesting. Actually," he said, standing, "I've been thinking about that kind of thing too." He held out his fist for a bump from Amos. "I'm off, dude. I'd say just tell her what you feel. It will promote cognitive and emotional health. Plus, you won't have any regrets when you die."

Amos nodded slowly. "This is very deep thinking."

"Nellie, can I talk with you a second?" Matt nodded toward the door.

I followed him, the churning in full force. I tried with all my intellect, a substantial force, to think of something witty or engaging to say, but when he turned to face me, I stared at his cheekbones. Right cheekbone, then left, then right again …

"Nellie, are you all right?" Matt looked concerned. He glanced at my mouth, which was open.

I shut it. "Yes, of course." I pulled my eyes away. "Just listening."

He narrowed his eyes. "Are you ill?"

I snorted, a decidedly unladylike response, but there it was. "No, no, not at all. You?"

He smiled slightly. "Um, no. In fact, I feel really good. The best I have in a long time. Nellie," he cleared his throat. "I want you to know that you're a really good friend to me. And I want you to be happy because, well, because you deserve it."

"Matt, I—"

"No, wait," he said. "I think I've been really annoying lately, and you've probably gotten sick of it. So I just want you to know that I'm over being annoying and now I'm ready to move into my Less Annoying Phase. Impossible, perhaps, given the raw material." He grinned.

I felt my heart drop to my toes. "I don't think you're annoying," I said, my voice rather mouse-like.

He shoved me on my shoulder. "Aw, shucks." He stopped when he saw my face unchanged. "Seriously, Nellie. Are you sure you aren't sick? Your cheeks are all pink and your eyes are fiery, like you have a fever or something."

I was breathing too fast. "Not sick," I said, leaning against the wall.

He watched me until I lifted the muscles in my face to reveal my teeth. Placated with the "smile," he pushed open the door to Margot's. "I'm off to read Freud. Mostly mindless blather, but the absolute most fascinating kind."

I nodded, keeping my teeth visible. I gripped the wall with my fingers, leaning my body against the glass of the door, and I watched him walk away.

22

Old Habits

Mrs. H. was singing when I got home. I don't think I can convey with words the shock this was. The woman did not sing. She did not dress in animal prints, she did not eat anything that came out of France, and she did not, ever, not once, sing in my presence. But there she stood, swaying to her own voice, her back to me as she mopped the marble floor in the foyer.

"Hello, young lovers, wherever you are," she sang. Mrs. H. never had children, but that was for the best. The breathy, fluttery vibrato alone would have made for some insurmountable lullaby issues.

I cleared my throat, and she jumped.

"Nellie, how many times have I told you not to sneak up on people!" She held one hand to her chest. "One of these days you're going to give me a heart attack."

"I wouldn't worry, Mrs. H.," I said as I tiptoed over the wet floor to the kitchen. "Young lovers hardly ever die of heart attacks."

She muttered a few choice words under her breath, which was reassuring. Second-chance love with Arthur DuPage didn't cause a total personality makeover. I slipped from the room as she sloshed water over the edge of her bucket and took to the floor with conviction. "Be brave, young lovers, and follow your star...."

Her voice faded from my hearing. I plucked a peach from a bowl on the butcher block and headed for the back stairs. The elder DuPage boy may have made Mrs. H. sing, but the younger was only rendering me mute and pink-faced. I sank my teeth into the flesh of the fruit, and my cheeks puckered, the peach was so perfectly ripe. Matt liked peaches. He liked peaches and blackberries and nectarines but not blueberries, and plums only if they were a bit sour. His second toe was longer than his big toe; so long, in fact, that it measured almost the same length as my pinky finger. He went through zealot phases with music and so listened exclusively to Phish, Cold Play, and James Brown at different points during high school. I knew all this trivia and more, but you didn't see me singing songs from *The King and I*. He'd moved on, if he'd ever even been within canoodling distance, which was doubtful. Nona might have been completely wrong about his feelings, and when I finally started coming to attention with my own, he was well-adjusted and reading Freud.

I paused for a deep breath when I reached the top of the stairs. The back door to Nona's attic was slightly ajar, and I pushed it with my elbow in order to spare it peach juice graffiti.

"Nona?" I called. "I'm home. May I come in?"

She turned from her canvas with a big grin. My heart soared: Today was a good day.

"Hello, Annette," she said. "Do you mind if I keep painting?"

I filled my lungs with air in an attempt to push the heartache out. “Go right ahead,” I said, taking a seat by the window. I watched her while I finished my peach.

The painting was new. The canvas had an all-over wash of pale indigo, and Nona was fussing with a set of hills that could have come from a Grant Wood. She’d brush with precise, quick strokes, then step back and take in the entire image. Then back to the same spot for more tweaking. I’d watched this process many times over the years and had marveled at her patience in creating just the right amount of light or dark, just the right texture or movement of the paint.

My eyes moved to her frame, the disheveled curls falling out of a loose bun, the oversized man’s shirt with splotches of paint littering even the back. She wore jeans cuffed to the calves, and if I’d asked a year ago, she would have argued for their rightful name, pedal pushers, instead of the newfangled and imprecise coinage, capris. Her shoes were a pair of Chuck Taylors, originally white but now the combined colors of hard work.

My eyes drifted to the periphery of the room. Nona had been busy. Paintings lined the junction of floor and wall, three deep in some places. I walked to a stack by the window and began flipping through. Wildly joyful some: bright swaths of red and orange, arcs of yellow, green, and fuchsia. Others were dark and mournful, barely eking out a smidge of light amid layers of black, blues, bruised purple.

Nona saw me looking. “Oh, Annette, honey, don’t look at those. I’ve got so much work yet to do. I just can’t seem to finish one before needing to start another these days.” She set down a narrow brush and picked up one with a robust plume.

“They’re beautiful,” I said. I paused in my riffling and leaned against the wall, legs crossed, one arm propped on a stack of clean canvases. "I think I've blown it, Nona."

"Oh, Annette, you were always far too hard on yourself," she said, not turning from her work. "It's good you chose that Clive Monroe. He seems like such a nice young man."

"He is a nice young man." Some things weren't worth the fight, proper nouns among them. "But I think I waited too long to figure out just *how* nice he is. I should have noticed when he was tortured and mopey and now, just when I want him to be mopey, he's all happy and focused and magnanimous. Magnanimous, from the Latin for *magnus* and *animus*, great or courageous of spirit."

"Hmmm," Nona said. She reached for a brush laden with goldenrod yellow.

"And then there's the Amish case."

"I knew an Amish girl once," Nona said, but stopped before adding any more.

"The Amish girl I know is about to make a big mistake. I'm trying to stop her, but I'm not sure it's going to work. And the Amish boy isn't making it easy, which makes me wonder how bad he wants it, you know?"

"A girl should only marry for love. Financial security is highly overrated."

That was the thing with this horrible disease or condition or whatever was robbing me of Nona. There were moments when she'd zone in on exactly what we were discussing, putting a name and face and context to my Amish boy and girl ill-fated but in love. And then, just as quickly, she'd be knee-deep in the murky waters again, wondering if she'd be late for her wedding or if Annette and Clive had had their baby yet.

"What should I do, Nona?" I said the words softly.

She turned, brush poised in her strong grip. "You do what we always do, dear. You cry or pout or laugh or whatever you must about what needs to be let go. And then you let go. Never try to run the world. Only a God of bottomless grace can pull off a feat like that."

I watched her return to her work, her spine straight and full of certainty. Those words, I knew, originated at a cellular level. Some things even a fractured mind could not erase. *Please God,* I prayed, not really knowing the end of that sentence. *Please.*

I returned to my perusal of Nona's work. A still life of peonies, her favorite flower. A landscape of the plains. My hands stopped their paging. A portrait of me, my undoctored afro hair, bright and curious eyes, a flush to my cheeks. I pulled the canvas and sat back on my heels. I was smiling in the portrait, as if it were a gift of an autumn day and I was just back from a meandering walk and would I like some cider and a hot doughnut? That kind of happy. The happy I had on my face when I smiled at my Nona.

She caught me staring and looked at the object of my gaze.

"Isn't she a lovely one?" she said and went right back to her painting. "I don't know that girl, but I dream about her face nearly every night."

The green backdrop, the russets of my hair, my smile, the eyes, they all blurred in my vision.

She still dreamed of me every night.

The world felt too heavy for me, and the one person who always knew how to lighten it was left with dreams alone.

Please.

23

Self-Defense

There was really no good reason I worked at an establishment dedicated to golf. The game itself bored me to the point of a nervous twitch by the third hole. I'd just as soon walk alongside a threesome, but only if the temperature read somewhere between 65 and 85. That Friday, it was 99 degrees with 90 percent humidity and not one single cloud in sight.

Visiting golfers not familiar with midwestern summers expressed confusion at these stats, wondering if perhaps they'd gotten the cloudless part wrong. Certainly there was an *ocean* of a storm brewing overhead with 90 percent humidity, they said. Certainly this girl must have her numbers wrong! How could a human survive such a harsh environ? I'll tell you how: unhappily. That's how she survived it. With a glare for anyone who dared to ask her a superfluous question, such as when the course closed (schedule posted on front door), where to find a restroom (sign overhead), or if it was going to rain (look at the ever-loving sky, buddy).

Oh, was I in a foul mood. To make matters less congenial, I'd gone shopping with Annette and was wearing one of the fruits of her labor. She'd been home for a few days that week and had pestered me about our shopping trip until I relented. After stops at the Willow Springs Mall, the line of boutiques downtown, and drive-bys at four separate strip malls, I'd returned to the house, stylish but depleted. For work that afternoon, I'd put on a sundress, "so flirty and fun" when in front of the three-way mirror in the store, but so overdressed and awkward at the course. Amos had whistled when I'd come in, and Tank had actually applauded, which had only irritated me more.

"You two, pipe down," I'd barked.

Amos laughed. "This is the perfect time for an idiom I have learned. Let me see: You can take the clothes out of the Nellie but not the Nellie out of the clothes." He slapped Tank on the back. "Yes? This is true, right?"

Tank chuckled but sobered up when he saw my face. "You look nice, Nellie. Not as nice as if you'd stop SNARLING like that, but pretty nice. Get ready for a BIG DAY. We're booked for tee times until closing."

Annette had told me taking better care of myself would make me less annoying at home. This was her gentle, maternal way of saying I was driving her nuts. I guess I'd been sulking. Normally Nona would have made me snap out of it, through words or a messy finger-painting session or an uncomfortably brisk walk around the neighborhood. I didn't have the heart to try any of those things without her, so instead I sulked. I'd gotten really quite good at it, carrying my cell phone everywhere and panicking aloud when it was out of sight. I walked with shoulders slumped, still the best way to get Annette riled up and begin the tirade about how I'd quit ballet too early. I'd even bugged Pop, normally unflappable, to the point that he'd snapped at dinner and asked me to stop sighing so much.

I figured that if Pop snapped, at least a halfhearted action must be taken, so I wore the sundress to work. It was long and flowy and scrunched all around the top to flatter what Annette had called "a small but feminine bosom." Not a word you wanted your mother to say, *bosom*. At any rate, I'd liked the dress before wearing it to the golf course. I thought about asking Tank if I could rip the tags off some of the athletic wear we sold, but we were so busy I didn't have the chance.

While I was ringing up two rounds for all thirty-two members of the Roggen Family Reunion, I saw my phone vibrate on the counter next to the register. The screen flashed "Claremont College." I felt a hard lump form in my throat and grabbed the phone as I retrieved eight cart keys for the Roggens.

The voice mail began with a pause, then a clearing of a throat.

"Nellie, this is Sonja Moss. I'm, well, I'm a bit perplexed. I ran into an Amish acquaintance of mine today at the farmers' market. Rose Lapp? We were discussing the differences between breeds of zucchini, and I was hoping I could convince her to let me have a look at her garden, but she laughed and said she thought one English girl picking up all the gardening secrets in one summer was enough. Of course"—big clear of throat here, a swallow of water or perhaps moonshine—"of course I wondered who this English visitor might be. She said—I swear she said the words *Nellie Monroe*, but then her daughter, a girl named Katie, changed the subject and soon enough whisked her mother off to churn butter or comb wool or some such excuse." She stopped abruptly. I pictured a reddening of the academic cheeks in the silence that followed. "At any rate," she continued, subdued, "I can't imagine I really heard your name. I can't imagine you would have been visiting an Amish farm, *my* Amish farm, without notifying me. Inconceivable, I would think. Anyway, would you mind giving me a call, Nellie? I'd appreciate hearing from you. This is probably just a matter of my poor hearing." She laughed a shrill, tinny laugh. "Do me a favor and call, won't you? Thank you, Nellie. Good-bye."

I handed the keys to Uncle Robert, the organizing Roggen, and hung up on voice mail. *That didn't sound good*, I thought. She was too close, and I was too close. It was time to make a move, and I knew just what to do.

The last reservation of the day was for a foursome, and I cringed when they walked in. All guys around my age, each wearing an incarnation of the same preppy baseball cap. The ringleader, a short, muscular man wearing a pink (pink!) polo shirt, leaned on the counter.

"Hey, there, cutie. You're a sweet cool drink on this miserable day." He winked at his friends.

"I'm sorry to have such a positive effect on you," I said breezily.

Pinkie looked confused. "No, babe, that's good. I mean, you look good." He checked me out over his sunglasses. I swear this happened, and it wasn't even a Molly Ringwald film.

"Right." I spoke slowly. I'd heard it worked well with primates. "But you're kind of leering, you know? And you're wearing so much cologne, I smelled you before I saw you. And you keep looking at my chest, which is socially inappropriate."

His buddies elbowed each other and snickered. I kept my eyes on his, darty and mole-like above the sunglasses. "Well," he said, "it would appear that an hourly wage doesn't offer the service it used to, is that right? Of course, showing skin like that, you might be better able to answer questions about a different kind of hourly service."

I pulled back and punched him square in the face. Let me assure you, this is nothing like it seems in the movies. First of all, there's no satisfying crunching noise. I listened, but nothing. Second, it hurts like the dickens. I cried out in pain, holding my hand and feeling hot tears fall down my face. Seeing blood on Pinkie's face and the looks of shock registering on his posse did comfort, but I'm telling you, it *hurt*.

Tank materialized without a sound, not a small endeavor for a man who considered any pizza without extra sausage "diet pizza."

"She hit me!" Pinkie pointed at my hand when he tattled. He added a whimper for good measure.

"I saw that," Tank said, and helped him to his feet. He turned him gently by the shoulders. "She gets a big bag of ICE and a RAISE."

"What?" Pinkie was frothing. His buddies followed behind, one clutching the big Italian sunglasses. "She needs to get fired, dude."

"NONSENSE. She saved me the trouble of hitting you myself. You tangled with the wrong girl, CHUMP." He opened the screen door but put a beefy finger on the guy's chest before he could step into the hot sun. "Listen up, kid." Tank spoke in a hushed voice, but I could still hear every word. "I'm not sure where you learned to talk to women like that, but pulling that kind of stunt around here will always earn you a bloody nose. Or worse. You GOT me?"

"Mm-hmm." Poor Pinkie. Not a good day to play eighteen holes.

"See you boys," Tank said, booming and cheery. "You have a nice AFTERNOON!" He let the door slam behind him and strode toward the ice machine. When he returned to the counter, he placed a full bag on my hand.

I flinched.

"Where'd you learn a move like that?" I could hear the smile in Tank's voice.

"Um, *CSI?* I haven't exactly tried it before." I sucked in air between my teeth. "Sorry about this."

"Are you kidding? That slimeball deserved more than a SMACK to the face. No one talks to my Nellie like that."

I could feel my eyes sting, just the kind of thing you don't want to happen when you've administered your first bloody nose to a perp.

"Now, now," Tank said, nudging me to sit on the stool behind the counter. He pulled up a chair and cradled my hand and the ice between his two mitts. "You go ahead and cry. It's allowed."

I sat, my hand sandwiched between his, letting hot tears wash down my face. Tank let me be and didn't say a word for a full five minutes. When I finally sighed, he sniffed. I looked up, and he was trying without success to stifle a laugh.

"MAN, I wish I'd had a video camera. He crumpled like a little girl, in his sweet widdle PINK SHIRT. Ha!" He slapped his knee with one hand and bumped the ice pack in the process. "Oh. Sorry." He shook his head. "I'd have loved to show a tape of that to your Nona in days gone by."

I allowed a half smile. "She would have approved, wouldn't she?"

"Oh, good gravy. She would have HOOTED and HOLLERED and then tracked him down to take a whack at him herself." His eyes searched mine. "She would have told you that God's the one who made you and so you'd better take his creation seriously. Don't mess with his best work, she would have said." He smiled, and I knew by the sadness in it how much he missed her too.

Amos stuck his head through the back doorway and froze. "Nellie Monroe! You have tears! What happened?" He hustled over to the counter.

"She's all right, Amos. Just had to PUNCH someone in the nose, that's all."

Amos took a look at my icing hand and clucked like an old woman. "Nellie, you will never find a husband if you can only punch and hit and kick. Men do not like this."

Tank snorted. "I'm not sure Nellie's in the MARKET for a husband just yet. Not quite the MARRYING type, right, Nel?"

I sat up straighter on my stool. "Yes, I am. I mean—" I'm not one who likes to stammer. It's unprofessional and irritating, especially for girls in sundresses. "I will, of course, be open to the idea when I'm a bit older."

Amos sniffed. "The English wait for these many years to be married and then their eggs are old and crusty. For example, the old women celebrities like the Courteney Cox, the Holly Hunter, the Helen Hunt, the Madonna (she is nasty), the Nicole Kidman, the Halle Berry, though she is delicious to view."

I shuddered and not because of the ice on my wound.

Tank hooted as he stood, patting my knee carefully before turning to go. I heard him reciting celebrity names as he made his way to the back of the store. "The Halle BERRY!" he said and let the screen door slam.

I tried my most intimidating glower on Amos. "First, puff pastry is delicious. Women are not."

Amos shook his head. "Oh, yes, they are—"

I held up my hand for silence. "Second, when and if I decide to marry is of no concern to you, crusty eggs and otherwise." My phone vibrated on the counter. Professor Moss again. I sighed. "Amos, I think my work for you is finished. I've solved your case, let you know what's going on with Katie and John Yoder, and I think it's time for me to bow out gracefully."

His eyes grew wide. "But what am I to do with Katie? How do I stop this wedding?"

I shrugged. "I'm afraid that's not covered in my fee. Besides"—I gave a small, tired smile—"I wouldn't know how to help with that anyway." I stood, biting my lower lip as my hand shouted out in protest. "But if you want my professional opinion?"

"Yes, of course. You are the best. I support you." Amos watched me with eager eyes.

I looked him full in the face. "Amos, if you love her, you need to act on it. The whole Amish thing does complicate matters, but you have to figure it out if you love that girl and want to marry her. She's inching toward a wedding with Slim Shady Yoder, so I'd hurry up if you're going to make a move."

His shoulders sagged but he nodded with great solemnity. "You are correct, Nellie. It is time for me to make a stealthy move. I have seen *Mission: Impossible,* and I know how to make these moves."

I stared at him, disturbed to the core to imagine him rappelling down into the Schrock barn in black tights. "Right. Well, you're on your own for that. But keep me posted." I held out my good hand to shake. "Thanks, Amos. It was a pleasure working with you."

His handshake was firm. "This is also my feeling, Nellie Monroe. Your future is bright in my opinion."

I smiled. "Thanks." I retrieved my purse and keys from under the counter. Halfway to the front door, I called back, "Keep me informed. I want to hear how it all turns out with Katie."

He waved, and I opened the door to the outside, never imagining how inextricable to his plot I already was.

24
Missing Persons

The next morning I hustled up the driveway to the Schrock house, taking care not to twist my ankle in the buggy-wheel ruts on either side. No rain for three weeks made for a dusty walk, but I kicked through the swirling clouds of dirt and took the stairs to the kitchen door two at a time. I hadn't returned Professor Moss's calls but knew my time of hide-and-seek was limited. The woman didn't seem like the type to get distracted by charm, and I considered my lying skills below average, so I would pay one last visit to the Schrocks and be on my merry way before the kettle got too hot.

Granny answered the door. "Nellie Monroe." She moved aside to let me pass.

"You look lovely today," I said, a glutton for abuse. "That shade of gray suits you."

She sniffed. "'The fear of the Lord is the beginning of wisdom,' and that is my focus."

I turned to close the door behind me and took the chance to roll my eyes. Couldn't she fear the Lord *and* look good in gray?

The kitchen was vacant, but I could hear a murmur of voices coming from the living room.

"Where is everyone?" I asked. "And is that … is someone crying?"

"Phst." Granny Mary shook her head and started for the door leading to the living room. "You are to sit and listen. Speak only if a person asks a question to you. Perhaps you can help the woman that cries."

I followed Granny into the spacious room. Wooden chairs and benches lined the perimeter, but only those gathered around the hearth were in use. I smiled what I hoped was a humble, antitechnology smile. Sarah's eyes met mine, and she beckoned me to stand near the semicircle of chairs.

The room fell silent as I crossed the room. I noticed John Yoder in the center chair, leaning forward with his elbows on his knees. He looked at me with a laser gaze, intent enough to give me a shiver in the heat of summer.

"Katie is gone," Sarah said quietly when I reached her side. "She did not come home the night before last." She gestured to the group and raised her voice a notch. "This is Nellie Monroe. She is the English girl learning to cook from Grandmother Mary."

I recognized Sarah's husband, Samuel, who nodded to me from where he stood by the mantel. John Yoder said nothing, staring at the cold fireplace. A middle-aged couple sat to his right. The woman looked over her handkerchief and attempted a pleasant expression. The man nodded in my general direction but made no eye contact.

"Katie's parents," Sarah said quietly. "Rose and Joseph Lapp."

John cleared his throat. "God forbid it, but she is injured. Or lost. She would not leave of her own accord."

Mrs. Lapp sniffed into her hankie. Mr. Lapp sat in stony silence.

Sarah took a deep breath before speaking. "Forgive me, but did she talk of discontent or worries about anything? The wedding perhaps?"

John stood abruptly and crossed his arms over his chest. He glared at Sarah. "No, she did not. Could not everyone see how happy she is?"

There was a moment of quiet. My heart raced. *Oh, dear, oh, dear,* I thought, recalling the plaintive smile Katie had summoned when telling me about her wedding dress. I tried to believe Katie was limping home with a broken arm, but all I could see was Amos and his goofy hairstyle.

"Nellie Monroe." Grandmother Mary barked at me from her station by the kitchen door. "It is possible we could use your help." I could see it pained her to say the words, so I kept my mouth shut out of respect. "We would prefer to keep this experience inside the family. Would you"—she stopped a beat and met eyes with Rose Lapp—"Can you help us to find Katie? She is probably in the world you know more about."

I recognized this comment as lightly veiled contempt. Granny Mary and I had some pastry-rolling hours under our belt, after all. From that time together, however, I could remember not one time when the Granster had asked anything of anyone, other than a glass of water or more lye soap to wash away the dirt of the world, literal and otherwise.

"I would be honored to help in any way I can." I could feel John Yoder watching my face. If there was one thing all my hours of PI prep had given me, it was the ability to stare anyone down, even strapping Amish men with surly expressions. Bring on the surly, I say. "I'd love to help you find Katie. And find out the truth."

As anticipated, John Yoder was the first to look away.

I sprinted to my car, hidden, as always, in the grove of trees near the road. On the way back to Casper, I stopped at Frank's Diner. Judging by Amos's euphoria over milkshakes, I could imagine him forcing Katie to try every one on the menu before they'd greeted each other with a holy kiss. Or any other kind of kiss for that matter.

A wash of air conditioning pulled me over to the counter. I scanned the booths, but the place was deserted during the mid-afternoon slump, not a slurping Amish in sight.

Frank himself peeked through the order window. "Nice outfit."

I tugged the strings on my bonnet until it gave up its battle with my hair and fell to the counter. "I'm, um, going to a costume party."

"In the middle of the afternoon?" Frank shook his head. "I'd wait until it was dark if I were you." He laughed at his own joke and went back to chopping something with a cleaver.

"Frank, did you see any Amish people in here today? Last night?"

"Nope," he said, not looking up.

"Are you sure?"

"I'm sure." He paused in the cleaver work. "What, Monroe? You looking for some friends so your costume isn't so sorry?" He pointed in the direction of the highway with his knife. "There are lots of 'em down the road. I'm sure they'd love to party it up with Miss Little House." This one got him laughing so hard, he began to wheeze.

"Thanks," I muttered and pulled open the heavy glass door. I'd wanted a Maytag burger to go, but a girl could only stand so much.

Two hours later, I had nothing to show for my efforts. I'd called Amos's cell eight times and had left increasingly irritated voice mails, the last three with paltry words: "Six." "Seven." "Message numero ocho." He could at least call, I thought. I mean, it wasn't like I'd lecture him. What he did with Katie was no business of mine. In fact, the more I drove around, stopping at his apartment, the golf course, his favorite McDonald's, the more offended I became. Worry wasn't on my radar. I knew to the fiber of my PI being that Katie and Amos were all right, probably canoodling somewhere by a lake, sipping virgin daiquiris. But the least the male lovebird could do was contact me. It was I, after all, who had kept the flame burning.

Tank answered my call as I pulled into the parking lot of Games Galore. "Any sign?" he asked. "That boy BETTER not have skipped town. I owe him money, and he owes me a finished mini-golf course."

"No word yet," I said. "I just pulled up to the arcade he haunts. I'll take a look." I swung my legs out of the car and stood to stretch. Audibly.

"For the love of PETE, Nellie. It's not exactly WINSOME to moan and GROAN like that, no matter how long you've been in the car."

I finished a hugely satisfying yawn. "Sorry, Tank. You let me know if he shows up, all right?"

"GOT it, sis. Take care, now. Never know what's going on under all that hair gel, you know? We don't know very much ABOUT that boy when it comes down to it."

I hung up, not having the heart to take away the drama from Tank, a man who watched *General Hospital* on rainy days at the course. Amos was an all-out prude when it came to illegal or risky behavior. I'd heard him lecture teenaged smokers about the dangers of nicotine and how he'd smoked his lungs to a crisp during his *rumspringa* but now suffered from asthma as a result. Once when we were cleaning out golf carts, he'd picked up a half-full can of Budweiser and carried it with pursed and prissy lips to the nearest trash can. He'd had enough, he'd said, during his "running around time," and the smell of it still reminded him of unfortunate mornings spent hugging the toilet.

No wild parties, I knew, so I scanned the dark interior of Games Galore while my eyes adjusted to the lack of light. A mangy teen stood at the front counter. He looked at me through a crop of bangs.

"Welcome to Games Galore, where fun is what we do best."

I couldn't help it. I was tired and hungry and miffed and my filter had eroded to nothing. So I laughed, really loudly and a bit too long.

Mangy Teen watched with droopy eyes. When I got it together, I straightened up and forced my mouth into a frown.

He stared at me through his hair. "Your nostrils flare when you laugh."

I cleared my throat and decided to ignore that comment. "Um, I'm looking for a semi-Amish guy. Medium height, muscular, wears lots of wild shirts, talks funny?"

He nodded once. "Amos. Yeah, I know him."

"Right! Amos. Have you seen him the last couple of days?"

He paused. "I saw him this morning. He came in wondering if we could sell him corn dogs to go, but we hadn't defrosted them yet. They're disgusting before we defrost them."

I saw a glass case of golden dogs turning behind him. I sighed and said, "I'll take one. With ketchup."

While Mangy Teen turned to get my order, I watched the goings on in Games Galore and could just imagine Amos getting riled up and yelling at the screens like some of the fourth and fifth graders next to me. A slight girl with cornrows was mopping up on Dance Dance Revolution while her mother talked on a cell phone. I took my first bite of the corn dog and regretted never asking Amos over for dinner. Food this rubbery could make a man drop off the grid without a moment's hesitation and take an innocent Amish girl with him.

I left the kid my name and number in case Amos came looking for breakfast again. The sun sank below a line of maple trees as I headed toward home and a real dinner. I would need my wits about me in the morning and a good night's sleep. Half a defrosted dog wasn't going to do it.

25

Prison Break

By seven the next morning, I was out the door and on my way to Margot's Coffee Nook for a quick shot to the system. I sat down with my caramel macchiato and took a deep breath while the coffee cooled. Settled into a chair by a window already perspiring with the day's demands, I made a mental run-through of where I'd been and where I was headed. One of the many gems I'd gleaned from StraightTalkWithSergeantJack.com was that organization was a private investigator's best friend. Sure, a high-speed chase through the alleys of downtown was an adrenaline boost. Stakeouts that involved the firing of weapons could get anybody's blood pressure up in a healthy way. But when it came right down to it, good work often relied on nothing more than a Venn diagram and a yellow legal pad.

Nona had always loved what she called God's mercy of morning. Everything looked better, felt better, and weighed less in the morning, she said. The night before, when I'd collapsed in exhaustion on my bed, I'd felt certainty slipping through my fingers. My sleep was fitful, myriad questions unnerving me even through my subconscious. *Maybe Katie isn't with Amos. Maybe she really is in trouble, just as John Yoder believes. I should call the police. This is too big for me. What if she's hurt and I'm wasting time on a chase? What do I really know about finding missing people anyway?* Doubt was my bedfellow, and let me assure you, he hogs the covers.

But the mercy of morning had renewed my determination to find Katie and my wobbly hope that all was well, albeit cloaked in secrecy. I made my list of potential stops and was tipping back the final dregs of coffee when my cell phone rang. I looked at the clock on the screen: 7:38. Two hours too early for Annette, Pop, or Matt. It was an unregistered number, but I picked up.

"Nellie Monroe?" Amos sounded wide awake.

"Finally!" I sounded just a hair this side of whiny, but I let him have it anyway. "Amos, I've left sixteen messages on your phone, and I've been looking for you everywhere—the arcade, your apartment, the diner—"

"Nellie Monroe, I am sorry not to call promptly. I am certain you know why I am not myself."

I let out a breath I must have been holding since the Schrock powwow. "So she's okay. She's with you."

He sighed with such dramatic contentment, I might have heard birds chirping. "Yes, she is most okay. And she is with me."

I rolled my eyes but allowed myself a smile. "All right, Romeo. I'll let you get back to your rocking chair or bundling or whatever you call it."

He gasped. "I take great offense to what you say, Nellie Monroe. We are not doing anything of those activities. Katie is pure as snow that is driven. I would never make her dirty snow."

It's a challenge to make snow an image of indignation, but he did it, to his credit. "I'm sorry," I said, a fresh wave of admiration for the two of them filling my chest. My tone softened. "I didn't mean to imply you would dishonor Katie, Amos. I know how much you care for each other."

"This is the truth," he said softly. "Thank you."

"I'll just head over to the Schrocks and let them know she's with you and not to worry."

"No! Do not tell anyone I have called you. We cannot—she cannot …" He seemed to be searching for the right words to string together. "We need more time. You cannot go to the farm or to Katie's parents and tell them we are together. The shock would be too much."

"The shock? Are you kidding? At this point they are worried their daughter is passed out somewhere with buggy tracks on her face. They asked me to help, Amos. The least I can do is tell them she's all right."

"No. No and no." I could imagine him shaking his spiky hair. "Nellie, you do not understand the Amish. If there is a rumor that Katie is alone with me, a male who is shunned, even though we know we have done no things to be raunchy, her image as a pure girl will be ruined. Her family will suffer."

I held my head in my hands, my thoughts reeling. "But they need to know the truth, and I said I'd help them. Their daughter is missing, and they're panicked."

"I know this. I will not take long before calling to you again. But please, Nellie. Please, give us time."

I couldn't remember hearing Amos sound this desperate, not

even in that first conversation on the playground. “All right,” I finally said. “I won’t say anything. But—”

“Thank you, Nellie Monroe! You are the greatest of Magnum PIs I have ever known.”

Tough to take that as a compliment, considering the source.

He continued. “If I am all alone in a dark parking lot and a bad guy jumps on me with knives or metal objects, I will call you to defend me! You are fierce!”

“All right already,” I said, allowing myself a moment of customer appreciation. “You’re being too kind.”

I heard a quiet female voice in the background, muffled by Amos covering the mouthpiece. “Nellie,” he said, “Katie says to thank you for everything and that she would eat anything you have baked before Granny Schrock’s food.”

I smiled. “She’s on.”

“She is on what? Right now she is not on anything. Right now she is standing by the door.”

It could get cumbersome, having a friend like Amos.

“You call me soon, got it?” I had my tough voice on again. “I’m serious, Amos. Don’t make me come for you.”

He giggled. “I do not ever want that, Nellie. You are a very scary broad.”

Amos, as usual, was completely off the mark in his assessment of me. I was not and had never been a very scary broad. Yes, I could drop-kick grown men and bring them to their knees. I made Amos scream like a little girl on more than one occasion. And that foul-mouthed frat boy deserved his broken nose. But with each hour I marked after my chat with Amos, the more I had to face the fact that I was all talk and no action when it came to being tough. In fact, I was one big-haired, cranky, freckled pansy, that's what.

The morning passed well enough. I'd racked up a list of past-due errands to run and groceries to gather what with my preoccupation with all things Amish. I hit Target, TasteWay, and the drugstore for Nona's refills all before noon. After a lunch of roast beef, provolone, and pickles on toasted focaccia, I went up to my room to read. The UPS man had brought my special order, a copy of *Love Is a Battlefield: A Private Investigator's Guide to Estranged Marriages*. I'd waited for that book for months, preordering it when I saw it reviewed in *PI Today*. Yet with the phone at my elbow irritatingly silent, I couldn't concentrate on what to do when a wife asks for copies of indicting transcripts or photographs. For a full hour I tried to get hooked on the words before me but to no avail. At last, I shut the book, grabbed my phone, and left the room.

I paced the house for a few hours, checking in on Nona, who was happy to be painting and didn't seem to notice if I was there or not. It did feel good to unload the whole story again, sparing no detail and with full confidence my words would never leave the cocoon of Nona's attic. When I'd talked through the peaks and valleys and Nona had said not a word in response, I headed downstairs and tried listening to Mrs. H. while she mooned over Arthur and his "way."

"We went dancing down at the Val-Air," she said, all girlish and pink in the cheeks. "And he has this *way*. I can't really explain it, but it honestly reminded me of Fred Astaire."

Puke.

"Last week he brought me a bouquet of irises because he knows they're my favorite flowers. He said these wonderful words about how indigo reminds him of me or something like that.… I can't remember precisely, but Arthur, he just has this *way.* The way he speaks, the words he uses.… It's a lot like Cary Grant."

Heave.

After the story of Arthur's *way* of washing cars, I had to take my leave. I'm all for true love, but there was a limit, and I think Mrs. H. crossed it about the time she brought up windshield-wiper fluid. Also, and much to my dismay, the mention of a DuPage man was making my heart feel sick. I needed to hit the road.

After an hour of aimless driving, I found myself heading toward the course. I pulled up slowly to the clubhouse, hearing through my open window the gravel crunching under my tires. On the sidewalk leading to the clubhouse, I passed a family of four in matching visors.

Tank called to them. "Have a GREAT time! Golf brings families TOGETHER!" He saw me approaching. "Did you find him?"

I shook my head. "Not exactly."

"How's the hand?"

I held it up for him to inspect. "Not bad. Purple skin is better than black."

He whistled. "I'm sorry you had to go through that. But MAN, was it worth it! To see that POSER'S face when you CLOCKED him good!" He slapped the counter as he laughed.

I plopped down like a ragdoll on a chair by the register.

Tank raised an eyebrow. "I'd say you were SICK, but you look well enough."

I sighed deeply and let my arms cushion my head's fall on the countertop.

"Well, now." The legs of the chair he commandeered protested noisily when he dragged them to sit next to me. "I suppose you should talk. TALK, not cry. I don't know if I can take crying." He cleared his throat.

I peeked through my forearms. He looked nervous.

"I'm not going to cry. Probably." My words were swallowed by the cave I'd built with my arms. I could feel my moist breath fogging up my face so I raised my head.

Tank coughed once, loudly. "Just so you know, kiddo, I'm not GOOD at this sort of thing like your Nona. Just don't want any high EXPECTATIONS for the old man in the GOLF SHIRT."

I smiled sadly. "I've made a mess, Tank. A big, honker mess."

"Honker? Well. That's the first time I've heard you use THAT word."

"Voluminous. Colossal. Byzantine. Mammoth. That kind of mess."

"First, does it involve MONEY?"

I screwed up my face.

"Good. Anything illegal? You don't have to answer that one, but I'd appreciate it if you did."

"No! Good gracious, Tank."

He held up one hand. "Last one: any UNPLANNED PREGNANCIES?"

I let my mouth fall open.

He nodded. "All RIGHT, then. How can I help?"

"I can't really tell you." What if Amos came hunting around the course and Tank betrayed that I'd told? It was too risky to involve anyone else, much less a man who shouted his words. "I can only say that I've woven a tangled web."

Tank sat forward in his chair and clasped his meaty hands, as if he were in a locker room during halftime and waiting for the plan for a third-quarter blitz. "You weave. WEBS. Help me out here, girl. I'm not one for CRAFTS."

"It's from a poem. 'What a tangled web we weave when first we practice to deceive.' I lied, Tank. And now some people are really hurting, and I can't tell them the truth because it's not really mine to tell."

"Well, that makes little or NO SENSE." He sat back in his chair. "But I can work with it. I do better with a LACK of specifics. These hurting people, do you care about them?"

I pictured Katie's parents, hunched over in grief; Sarah Schrock, her arms pulled tight around her waist, sadness in her eyes. I felt my heart sink, picturing them going about their daily work without knowing if Katie was safe or even alive. Even grouchy Granny, her eyes sharp with concern, made me feel pangs of regret and compassion. "I do. I really do. I didn't mean to, but I didn't mean for most of this to happen the way it did."

"Again, GREEK to me. But I'll say this: Until you tell the truth to these people, you're going to be miserable, and it sounds like they will too. Now, it's one thing if it's a secret that's not yours to SPILL. It's another, though, if you're keeping your own secret and hurting them while you do it."

I fiddled with a carton of gum sitting next to the register. *My secret to tell …* I had plenty to disclose to the Schrocks without even dipping into Amos and Katie's current dilemma. I picked at the cellophane wrapper and thought of that big farmhouse, its open rooms, the inability for so much as a fleck of dirt to hide. A not-so-quiet nudge hit me in the gut: *Time to sweep out the corners.* Time, as Nona would say, for some truth telling.

"You gonna BUY that, girl?" Tank jabbed toward the packet of gum, nearly unwrapped under my meddling fingers.

I tried a fetching smile. "Do I get a discount?"

"BAH." He shoved back his chair and rose, cracking both kneecaps as he stood. "On the house." He let out a satisfied, low whistle. "By the looks of your EYES, I'd say my work here is done—skeedoodle." He raised one hand for a five. "Hit me."

I slapped five and then jumped up to hug him. When I pulled back, he looked surprised, pleased. "Thanks, Tank," I said and stood on my toes to kiss him on the cheek. "You did great."

"That RIGHT?" I wouldn't say he blushed, but he would have if he hadn't already been sweaty.

"And don't tell her," I lowered my voice, "but you gave Nona some stiff competition."

He hooted and slapped the counter. I nearly skipped to my car, the sweet taste of freedom already on my lips.

26

Nothing but the Truth

"And so," I said to the air conditioning vent in my car, "I hope you understand how sorry I am and that you can forgive me. Your people, if I may be so bold, can understand better than most what it's like to want something that no one else understands." *Too chummy*, I thought, flicking the vent with my finger. I'd parked around the bend from the entrance to the Schrock farm and was putting the final touches on my apology speech. The more I practiced, the more nervous I became. I hitched up my stockings and turned off the car. Pulling my hair into a loose bun, I stuffed on my bonnet and got out to face the music. Or *a cappella* singing, as the Amish weren't fond of instrumentation.

I muttered to my feet as they booted a rock in fits and starts down the driveway. "It was never my intention to hurt anyone, but I know now I should have been honest." So deep inside the finer points of groveling was I that I didn't look up to see the parked cars until I was nearly to the front porch. One battered looking Saab sat behind an impeccably cared-for Jag, sapphire blue, spotless, and bearing an uncanny resemblance to my father's. My stomach dropped. I paused by the car and stared up at the screen door. No sound was coming from within so I tiptoed up the stairs. When I peeked into the kitchen, Granny's face appeared, eyeball to eyeball with my own.

I screamed.

She frowned but then moved away without opening the door.

Sarah came from behind and pushed on the door without meeting my eyes.

Clive and Annette sat at the kitchen table, looking coiffed, tanned, wealthy, and miserable. I was sure Annette would have tossed around a few bangles and beads to the women in the room if they had accepted them. And given them haircuts. She always said a woman needed to know when to let go of long hair. She caught my eye, and I thought she was about to cry.

The other car, I realized, belonged to Professor Moss. She approached me quickly and nodded. "Hello, Nellie. We've been waiting for you to arrive. Were you always late for your appointments with the Schrocks?" Her chin was quivering, but it didn't strike me as a scared quiver. More of a wish-I-could-poke-your-non-PhD-eyes-out quiver.

"No," I said in a small voice.

Granny Mary said something under her breath in Pennsylvania Dutch, and I did not feel the need to ask her to clarify.

"You're probably wondering how we all came to be here." Professor Moss mopped her upper lip with a tissue. In the depth of summer, the woman was still the picture of Nordic paleness. I could see purple veins crisscrossing her cheeks. She continued. "When you wouldn't return my calls, I decided to pay a visit to your home. Your mother and father had no idea what to make of your unanswered voice mail and of the rumor I'd heard about your involvement in the Amish community this summer. But then, as luck would have it, your grandmother came downstairs."

Oh, how Nona would disagree with that statement. No such thing as luck, she'd say, except in blackjack and bra size.

"What a help she was! She told us all about what had been happening with the Schrocks, who was who, which one is the best cook, what you'd been learning, and how you'd been spying—spying!—on this poor family without their knowledge in order to gather personal information that was none of your business." By this time, Professor Moss was shaking enough that she had to lean against the wall. Sarah came to offer her a chair and a glass of water.

I took the opportunity to begin my speech. I hadn't planned on giving it to such a large and bizarre audience, but there it was. My Pop met my gaze from his position at the table. He nodded slightly. I exhaled.

"It was never my intention to hurt anyone here, but now I can see I should have been honest. Or at least partially honest. Maybe not at the beginning with Professor Moss, since I needed her to get to you, but at least with, for instance, Katie. Or Sarah." I had never been one for public speaking. During the Romeo and Juliet unit in ninth grade, I'd ended up telling a story about my cat that died from eating all the World's Finest Chocolate candy bars I was supposed to sell for a band fund-raiser. I really should have made an outline on index cards.

Professor Moss pursed her lips.

"Let me try that again." I spoke quickly. "First and most important, I'm sorry. I'm sorry I made this mess and that I betrayed the trust each of you offered me." My heart was beating wildly, and I clenched my hands at my sides in an effort to keep from running. "It's true that I came here on false pretenses, but that's not how things ended up. I was hired to gather information on the part of a friend."

"Amos Shetler! This boy is not a friend! He is outside the church!" Granny stopped short when Sarah put a hand on her arm.

"I know. But he loves Katie, and he just wanted to know what was happening with her." I moved a step toward Granny and held out my hands. "Grandmother Mary, I know you understand what it means to love people so much it hurts. Your mean face and harsh words are nothing compared to the way you love Sarah and Elizabeth and your son and your grandchildren. I've seen it hour after hour. You're a really bad faker."

Granny swallowed hard and looked at the ceiling.

"And Professor Moss, I'm very, very sorry to have used your work for my gain. I was trying to be good at my job, but it was unfair of me to keep you from doing yours. If it's any consolation, I fully understand now why you are so protective of this family and why you want to spend as much time as possible with them."

"That consoles me not in the least," she growled. Turning her face away, I could still see the anger in her profile. "The least you could have done was share," she added, her voice a shade smaller.

Not many would ask to share the Amish fun, but I should have known Moss would. I'd stolen her hard-earned research, and now I felt like an academically degenerate heel.

I turned to my parents and sighed. "Mother, Pop, I'm just sorry you were dragged in. Not very luminary-like behavior." My words caught in my throat and big, salty tears threatened to make their way down my cheeks. I saw my mother blur in my line of sight as she stood up from her chair and walked to my side. I buried my face in her shoulder, and she rubbed my back.

"I wanted to show you I could do it," I said into her armpit.

"You can do anything you want, and that's the truth." She said the words quietly, but the conviction behind them made me catch my breath. She tried to smooth my hair under the bonnet, and I could feel her rummaging in her pocket for lip gloss, but at that moment, she could have injected me with Botox, I was so grateful to have her hugging me, showing all those who doubted that I had a mother's love, at least.

After a moment, Granny Mary cleared her throat. I moved out of Annette's embrace to face the woman and the scowl.

"You are no longer welcome in our home, Nellie Monroe." She turned and walked out of the kitchen.

I felt like I'd been kick-boxed right in the gut. I heard Elizabeth, bless her, sniffling over by the window. My mother put a hand on my shoulder while tears paved impatient thoroughfares down my cheeks. Sarah moved to me and took my hand in hers. She led me, my mother, and my father to the door, her steps careful and her grip warm in my hand. When we reached the screen, she squeezed my hand once before opening the door for us.

"I'm sorry," I whispered. "I was wrong. Sarah, I'm—"

Sarah shook her head. "I see your sorrow, Nellie." She held the door open. "Godspeed."

To the contrary, my feet could not have been more anchored to the earth as they made a path to the car.

I'd always admired the Roman tradition of reclining while eating. That night, as I lay on my back on Nona's hardwood floor with a plate of Havarti and Triscuits on my chest, my admiration deepened—because it was much more difficult than it looked, let me tell you. I propped my head on a sofa pillow, which helped. But I remained within easy striking distance of a Havarti slice sliding onto my tear-puffed eyelids, a minimal act of justice considering my transgression.

"Maybe I should take up macramé," I said through a cracker. "Nona, you always said I was artistic."

Nona smiled at me and patted my head, just as she'd done for the last hour. "You're a sweet girl, you know that?"

"Thanks," I said, "but that's not entirely accurate." A crumble of cheese landed on my chin. "Okay, maybe not macramé. How about sewing? I made a fleece pillow in eighth grade. Smoked that final exam, I'll have you know."

Nona patted my head. "I love spring, don't you?"

I nodded and handed her a cracker, which she took and studied for a moment before stacking it on the coffee table with the others.

"I'm really not into anything athletic. Or the outdoors. Too many bugs and things that could nibble on toes. Ooh!" I turned my head toward Nona, which meant I was nose-level with her jeans. "I could move to Burbank and be a game-show contestant! I would scorch *Wheel of Fortune*. And if I could get on the high school version of *Jeopardy!*, I'd make *bank*." I took a deep breath and heard it catch like a machine gun, still shaky after all the crying I'd done since leaving the Schrock house. When I'd get control, I'd hear Granny

Mary's sentencing reverberate in my head and get all riled up again. Nona was unsure of why I kept at it, but she wouldn't leave my side, patting my head and talking about springtime. Close enough, I thought, and stuck to her like glue.

A decisive knock sounded on the door. Strange, I thought as I scrambled to a seated position. No one in my family sounded that sure of themselves unless they were entertaining. I walked to the door and opened it to Matt DuPage, the one and only. A wave of nervousness flipped over in my stomach.

"Matt."

"Nellie." His eyes were kind but a little sparky. It was the spark that made me bite my lip. "Can I come in?"

I moved aside for him to enter. He crossed the room to Nona and deposited a kiss on her forehead. "Hi, Nona. It's me, Matt."

She looked up at him and smiled. "Oh, of course. You're the gem around here."

I did not take offense, but I did shake my head. Somewhere in there, she still knew him and how great he was.

He turned to me and nodded toward the two chairs by the window. "Can we talk?"

I followed, worrying my bottom lip about what he might say and what I might say back. It was one thing to confess one's failings in a professional arena. All right, so it wasn't really very professional, what with the weeping and the costume and the presence of my parents. Nevertheless, I had opened the honesty floodgates already that day, and I was concerned they weren't closed and airtight enough to be sitting in comfortable chairs across from the repressed love of my life.

"It's good to see you." Matt's grin made my heart race.

"Good to see …" I mumbled in return. Not the strong start I'd hoped for, but I was thinking less was more in terms of words spoken.

He punched me on the thigh. "I've missed you."

"I love you!" The words just flew out of my mouth and landed right, square between us. I stood. "Sorry. I need to go." *Could this* get *more awkward?* I thought. *Perhaps I should sit on his lap and start singing "Time After Time" by Cyndi Lauper! That'd kick it up a notch! Or maybe I should shimmy! To a drumbeat played by Nona! Much less horrifying than simply blurting out a confession of love to an unsuspecting friend.* Argh!

I started for the door, not really thinking of where I could go to escape other than not in the attic with Matt. He ran around me and blocked the door with his body. I could have taken him, but I was all out of fire for the day.

His eyes were shining. "Did you just tell me you loved me?"

I sighed. "Probably not. You probably heard something wrong. Like the wind."

"The wind." He appeared to be considering this. "The wind spoke in your voice and told me you loved me."

"That's what I'm thinking."

"Dang." He frowned.

I narrowed my eyelids and wondered if he could see my heart leaping out of my chest. "Clarify 'dang.' Is that a regretful 'dang' or a 'Dang, she's one messed-up girl to hear the wind speaking English'?"

One side of his lip curled into a smile. "Equal parts regret and you're messed up."

I watched him, my breathing so shallow, I saw little prickly stars start to fall around us.

He moved one step closer to me, which put him within kissing distance, a measure I'd become suddenly very keen on noticing. One kissing distance minus one kissing distance would equal his very perfect and pink lips on mine. A veritable meteor shower began, and I forced myself to breath more deeply.

"Nellie," he said, shaking his head slightly, "I started loving you the day we both fell out of the oak tree in my backyard and we limped with arms around each other's shoulders to get ice from the kitchen. I loved you when you wrestled Pete Ollinger behind the school and ended up losing so miserably, you made me count your fifty push-ups every afternoon until the rematch. I loved you when you went to homecoming with that idiot Scott Jaarsma and he left you at the dance with nothing but an ugly flower on your dress. I loved you when we spent the last night before college roasting marshmallows over the fire pit in your backyard and making each other cry, we laughed so hard. Nellie." He planted himself in front of me, completely erasing the kissing distance. Kissing distance zero! "You are so unbelievably weird."

Um.

I cocked my head. "The words every girl longs to hear."

"Seriously. You are crazy. Nutso. And really kind of irritating."

"Are you going to rein this in? I'd like you to rein this in."

He tucked a strand of frizz behind my ear.

"I didn't flatiron," I said testily.

"See?" He laughed. "What the *heck* is a flatiron? And why would you use it when you're already beautiful with your huge, insane hair?"

All right. I melted. "You think that?"

Kissing distance restored to zero. "Like I said." He kissed me on the cheek, softly. "I've loved you since." His kiss, the first and sweetest, made every multisyllabic word leave my head. It was a kiss to defy Webster, that kiss.

When he pulled away, I said, "I love you, too."

He rolled his eyes. "Took you long enough."

At six o'clock the next morning, my phone rang, and Matt's number showed up on the screen. I rolled over to snatch it from my bedside table.

"Are you going to call this early now that we're kissing? Because I'm really going to hate that."

"Morning, cupcake."

"And also I hate terms of endearment."

"How about muffin? Duck? Lambkin? Cuddles?"

"I just want to be friends."

He did have a nice laugh, but it was still too early.

"Listen, kitten, I think I can help you clean up the mess you've made for yourself. Amos called me and wanted some help with a few woman questions. Clearly he understands the best source for that kind of information." He made a sound like he was hitching up a horse or maybe spitting tobacco. "Want to go with me to pay a visit to the Amish Don Juan?"

27

As Good as It Gets

We stopped at TasteWay on the way to the address Amos had given Matt.

"I still don't understand why he told you and not me where they were staying." I was pouting as we filled a flat of sour cream doughnuts.

"I have superb people skills." Matt tossed in a few doughnut holes. "You really should delegate that part of your business to me. The people part."

I karate chopped him in the gut but gave him a kiss on his smooth-shaven cheek, then migrated toward his lips.

Misty Warren-Pitz cleared her throat. "Hello, public display. First of all, I didn't even know you were dating, and secondly, it's early and the baked goods section."

"You're right," Matt said. "We should have the decency to kiss in the cereal aisle. Or by household cleaners."

Misty narrowed her eyes and turned to me. "Word to the wise: Live your life before you're stuck with a husband and kids." She gestured to her growing belly. "Keep kissing like that, and you'll have one of these to carry around with you." A chocolate éclair in one hand, she stomped off to find that poor Pitz man.

Matt pulled one hand around my waist as we walked toward the register. "She's so inspiring. I was all ready to propose Vegas this weekend, and now I think maybe that would be rushing it. What do you think?"

I laughed. "I think you're funny. And very attractive for someone who used to have a pronounced stutter. But I still don't appreciate Amos confiding in you instead of me. You're not *that* great."

"Aw, thanks, poopsy."

That time, the gut punch did not follow with lip action.

The dive where Amos and Katie had been staying sat at the bottom of a hill on the east side of town. When we'd settled in the living room on a beat-up couch and two folding chairs, I took stock.

"Amos, this is a dump." A bit harsh, perhaps, but I was nursing a wound.

"Yes, it is revolting," Amos said. He looked around at the peeling paint, the stained carpet, a duct-taped window. "But no one found us here. My friend Steve let us stay here without requiring money. This is a good thing."

I looked at Katie. She sat next to Amos on the couch, her hands cradling a paper plate with a nibbled-at doughnut. I'd expected her to be dressed in jeans and a T-shirt. Instead she wore the same clothes she wore to work at the Schrock farm. The only difference was a long braid down her back instead of the traditional pinning-up.

"You look nice, Katie," I said, smiling. "Are you doing okay?"

She nodded and took another nibble of her doughnut while she thought. "I am well, thank you, Nellie. I know my family will never understand, but I believe I needed to do this. To go to the outside and stay with Amos."

Matt leaned forward in his chair. "I think you're both brave." He looked embarrassed. "For what it's worth."

Amos offered his fist for a knuckle bump. "Thank you, buddy. Maybe brave, maybe stupid, but Katie is correct. We needed to talk in this apartment for some days."

Katie sat up straighter on the collapsing cushions. "We have made decisions. I want to be Amish. I want to be myself, and that is Amish."

"All right," I said softly. "So Amos will return with you?"

Amos turned to Katie and took her hand. "I want to be myself too. And my own self is a wild thing to make your heart sing."

Matt raised his eyebrows. "Really?"

"Yes," Amos said, nodding soberly. "I'm living *la vida loca*. I cannot return to the Amish because that is not who I am." His shoulders pulled downward. "The unfortunate circumstance is that Katie and I cannot be together with this plan."

She leaned over and gave him a light kiss on his cheek, which provoked a deep blush from Amos's gelled hairline to his stubbled chin. He frowned at his shoes.

Katie looked at his profile while she spoke. "We will always care for each other. Amos Shetler is a good, good man, and this is the truth." Her voice caught, and I saw Amos squeeze her hand. "But we cannot be honest to us and to what we want if we force one of us to be what God did not intend."

The room was heavy. I took in the mourning on Katie's face and wanted to throw myself at Matt and hug his neck for gratitude that he wasn't a part of a closed religious sect, so grateful was I not to be enduring this kind of torture. Matt hunched over in his seat, eyes downcast.

"Do not be depressed, dude." Amos's voice was sober but strong. "We know this is the right action, though it is not the first choice."

"Amos is right," Katie said. "And because I have had this time to think, I know to my heart that I cannot marry John Yoder."

"This is awesome," Amos added, "because he is a piece of scum from a pond."

"Amos," Katie warned.

"Sorry," he muttered but didn't look very apologetic.

Katie let go of Amos's hand and smoothed her skirt. "So I will need a ride back to my home, please." She met my eyes with clarity and resolve in hers. "Nellie, will you come with me to the Schrocks? I know my parents will be there, and I want everyone to hear my defending words of you."

"I'm not very popular around there right now," I said, fear prickling the back of my neck at the mere thought of Granny.

Katie sighed. "Neither am I." She stood. "If we go together, perhaps they will not kill two people."

Matt and I stepped out to the car to let Amos and Katie say good-bye. Amos wanted to go back with Katie and, as he said, "Be the large man about conflict resolution." Katie insisted this was not his battle to fight and it would be best if he stayed out of it.

"Where did he learn the phrase *conflict resolution?*" I asked.

Matt popped the trunk to place Katie's near-empty bag inside.

He let the door drop and grinned at me. "I finally found a friend who will read the books I recommend."

I pointed my finger at him when he approached. "That's another thing that won't change because we're locking lips. No early-morning love calls, no Princess or Angelface, and no reading self-help books. Got it?"

He turned with me and faced the door of the apartment building, watching a tear-stained Katie emerge. "We have it really good," he said before opening the door for me, then Katie.

Did we ever.

28

Grace Sufficient

Katie and I stood at the weeping willow in the Schrocks' front yard. We faced the house together, watching the white clapboards mellow to indigo as night began to fall. The cicadas belted out throaty blues, their songs cascading into each other without pause. After a stop at Matt's house, where we'd left him and his promises to pray like Nona would, Katie had blurted out a last-minute request for Frank's. She'd poked around her cheeseburger and fries and let most of her strawberry malt puddle in the bottom of the metal glass.

When I had tucked the receipt into my purse and scooted to the edge of the booth seat, I asked if she was ready.

"It feels good, like deep water in my heart to go back home. Yet I know that I have hurt the people there." She tucked a strand of blonde into her *kapp*. "People are fragile. I will need to be patient with the healing."

We stood under the willows, the leaves brushing our arms and shoulders, and I thought of John Yoder. Before Katie's comment, I would not have pegged John Yoder as one who struggled with fragility. Bad table manners wouldn't have been a stretch. Or a man who might overuse the phrase *women's work*. These were all conjecture; I hadn't had the opportunity to break bread with John and discuss the forward progression of feminism. But she was right, Katie was. John Yoder, with all his bravado, was fragile, as fragile as I was or Annette was or Misty Warren-Pitz, for that matter. We were all in need of mercy and patience with the binding up after things had been torn to pieces.

She knocked once on the kitchen door, and Sarah answered before we could take a full breath. When her eyes met with Katie's, I saw them fill. The door creaked to its greatest width as Sarah pulled Katie into her strong arms. I heard snippets of Pennsylvania Dutch as the two women reconnected. I, however, took great interest in the potted geraniums at my feet. *I should have dropped Katie at the end of the lane*, I thought, frustrated anew that I was the foreigner back for more emotional flogging.

"Nellie," Sarah said, arms still around Katie, "you should come in."

"No thanks," I said, chipper as a talk-show host. I smiled, with my bottom row of teeth thrown in, and said, "I was just leaving. I'm not really dressed—" I gestured to my flip-flops and jeans.

Sarah looked confused. "You are English. English girls wear denim and flimsy sandals."

So my efforts at cultural assimilation had failed as well. Chalk it up.

Granny appeared in the doorway. She took one look at Katie and said, "I will talk with you now, Nellie Monroe." Have you heard a dog growl? Same timbre, same warning bells.

I followed Sarah and Katie, who walked together behind Granny. Sarah's husband, Samuel, and their three teenaged sons sat at the table over a pitcher of lemonade. They fell silent when we entered. Granny said something in rapid-fire Pennnsylvania Dutch, and they shoved back from the table and retreated to the living room. She moved to the seats they vacated and took one without offering the others to us.

Katie cleared her throat and distanced herself slightly from Sarah. "Grandmother Mary, Sarah, I want to say my apology for the worry I have created. I will have many apologies, too, for my parents and for John Yoder." She paused and took a deep breath. "I cannot expect you to understand why I needed to leave, but I did. And I am home now and ready to be who God has intended for me."

"Good." Granny said, with a soft stomp of her foot on the wooden floor. "Your parents deserve honesty. You will go there now?"

"I will," Katie said, standing a half-inch taller. "I want first to talk with you about Nellie."

"There is no need," she said, lifting her chin. "I can speak with her myself." She looked at me with the tenderness of a gargoyle. "Come to me."

Why, oh, why aren't I home? I thought. The elderly woman at *my* house didn't hate me and speak condemning words in archaic languages. I padded toward Grandmother Mary, my hands clenched and sweaty at my sides, my cheeks already burning with shame. I'd brought back the could-be-dead Amish girl, darn it. Didn't that count for anything? Judging by the fire in the Granster's eyes, I didn't think so.

"Nellie Monroe, you have sinned. You did not tell the truth, which steps over the ninth commandment. Even heathens can sometimes obey those ten." She sniffed. "Also, you have brought trouble into this house and into Katie's house that would not have come without you. You opened a box that had shut, and this is not wisdom."

I hung my head, the truth bearing down on my spine. My toes peeked out on my flip-flops and even they looked pathetic, the nail polish chipped and halfhearted. I was a hunk of pathetic, dishonest, Amish destruction, that's what.

"But"—and she hesitated—"I forgive you."

I looked up, waiting for the ultimatum or the second verse of the chastising song. I waited for what I deserved, and she said nothing. She looked me full in the face and watched my tears falling hard and fast on her scrubbed wooden floor, and she nodded slowly. Stubborn grace, it turned out, came in various forms, straight from the hand of God and in the form of a cranky old lady in a bonnet.

29

Days of Plenty

Nona sat with me in the kitchen booth, sipping a steaming cup of mango peach tea while I worked on my coffee. I'd cracked open one of the lead-glass windows to let in the morning air. We'd hit the first days of September, and a delicious bite of crisp came with both the sun's rising and its ever-quickening descent.

"How is your tea, Nona?"

She looked up at me and smiled. "I've never been to Scotland. Have you?"

I shook my head. "Not yet."

"Not yet," she repeated, sipping from the china cup as daintily as a lady-in-waiting. In the web of memory and imagination and melancholy and confusion that had occupied her mind, maybe today a lady-in-waiting made perfect sense.

I drank deeply from my cooling cup, savoring the warmth as it traveled through my fingers, across my palms. From my seat across from her, I watched Nona. I'd helped her pin back her hair, letting some wisps of white frame her face in the way it would have were she to spend the morning painting instead of moving to Fair Meadows. Her eyes were a ferocious blue at such an early hour, nearly jarring in their intensity of color. Every few moments she'd remembered my presence and would smile or tip her head to one side and say whichever words seemed immediate and pressing.

"I tried impatiens in that flat near the patio, but there just wasn't enough shade. Begonias did much better."

"Nona, you are really beautiful." The words didn't pain me because they couldn't have been more true.

"I once wore a bright red strapless gown to that dance hall. Probably overdressed, but I loved the feel of that gown."

Our conversations tended toward these tangents as of late. Her mind would make a loop toward when she'd felt beautiful, but she couldn't complete the circle to where I stood in the present, her granddaughter, red-haired and freckled and waiting to hear her say my name.

"Nona," I said, covering her hand with mine. "I want to tell you some things."

She looked out the open window. A cardinal perched on the back porch railing, preening in his reflection in the glass.

"I'm going to be okay." The words caught in my throat but I took a deep breath and began again. "For one thing, I'm ready to go back to school this fall. I'm going to keep taking my criminal justice classes, and I'm working on an internship with a Cleveland law firm. Using fancy words to catch bad guys might be right up my alley. But"—I paused, brushing an errant grain of sugar from the table—"I might just surprise you too. Now that I've learned how to make a mean pastry crust, I might have to open my own bakery."

"Casper can be a tough place to live. When we got back from Italy in 1990, Annette wanted nothing more than a loaf of crusty bread." She giggled. "That woman in the Cascade Bakery said, 'Well, why don't you just let it sit out overnight?'" She laughed, a real bell-like laugh that came right from the middle of her.

I laughed, too, holding on to that story she'd shared with me many times before she got sick. "I might learn crusty bread. Or maybe I'll just head right through to an MBA and run my own bakery by day, PI agency by night."

I picked up the small blue delft pot between us and filled Nona's teacup.

"Also, I'm not going to lie to any more Amish people. Or professors." I shuddered. "That Sonja Moss is one impossible woman when crossed. I think I'm up to about hour twenty of the hundred she's asked that I serve in penance for delaying her research. So far I've alphabetized her files, bought and organized four new bookshelves, and fertilized all her dying ferns back to life." I raised my eyebrows in conspiracy. "I'm pretty sure I'll be able to wear her down until she lets me come along to the Schrocks. They liked me better anyway."

Nona tapped on the window. The cardinal cocked his head to one side but didn't fly away. She looked at me.

"Also, you should know that I've been thinking about God."

Her eyes crinkled with what looked like joy to me. Like she'd just happened upon a tree with lights and ornaments and a whole slew of wrapped presents.

"I don't have a lot to say about him yet. Just thought you'd like to know." I swallowed hard. "He's kind of persistent, that's one thing I've noticed. And when I try to think he's not interested in me or that he might be the stuff of nursery rhymes, all I can see is your face and how you looked when you talked with him or about him." I was crying.

She closed her eyes. "'I am still confident of this: I will see the goodness of the Lord in the land of the living.'" Her face was smooth, remarkably so after enough years of sun and life and worries and pain and laughter to break a thousand surfaces. "I love that psalm."

I held her hand, knowing that Matt would be there any moment with his able hands to carry Nona's last suitcase and his expansive heart ready to help me put one foot in front of the other. I knew Mother and Pop would meet us at the doors of Nona's new home, where there would be fresh flowers on the table and too many throw pillows added by Annette's decorator. I knew Nona would be well cared for and that she would see me every single day and that she might not know either of those things for more than a moment at a time. I knew that she was right and that the writer of that psalm was right, and that before I got to be old and holding my granddaughter's hand, I would understand those words too.

The cardinal tipped his head and sang a throaty, exuberant song before flying away. We watched him go, his wings revealing an entirely different wash of color with the upward arc of his body. The effect was sublime, from the Latin of "to elevate," meaning causing astonishment or wonder.

It's not a word to be used often, but in that moment, it was a perfect fit.

... a little more ...

When a delightful concert comes to an end,

the orchestra might offer an encore.

When a fine meal comes to an end,

it's always nice to savor a bit of dessert.

When a great story comes to an end,

we think you may want to linger.

And so, we offer ...

AfterWords—just a little something more after you

have finished a David C Cook novel.

We invite you to stay awhile in the story.

Thanks for reading!

Turn the page for ...

- **Letter from Sergeant Jack Knight**
- **Grandmother Mary's Rhubarb Pie**
- **A Final Word from Amos Shetler**

Sergeant Jack Knight

P.O. Box 8369 • Muskogee, OK 74401

www.StraightTalkWithSergeantJack.com

Dear Ms. Monroe,

Thank you for sending along a copy of your term paper, "Ohio Old Order Amish: A Sting Operation." I found the section regarding ethnic profiling to be particularly interesting.

I'm pleased to hear my online course has helped you in your pursuit of investigative mastery. Don't miss my upcoming release *Take Back the Knight Before Someone Else Takes It First* (Knight Rider Press). The chapter on facial intimidation might be of interest.

One case at a time,

Jack Knight

Grandmother Mary's Rhubarb Pie

Note from transcriber:

I could not offer enough worldly compensation, bribery, or pitiful begging to get Granny's permission to print her crust recipe. She said if you want it, you'll need to set up an appointment but that she limits her cooking lessons for foreigners to once a year.

Good luck with that.

In better news, this filling for a rhubarb pie is fantastic and, as Mary put it, "Easy enough for even an English know-everything." Count yourself blessed. –N.A.L.M.

Ingredients:

3 cups rhubarb, diced
1¼ cups sugar
2 heaping tablespoons flour
2 tablespoons butter, cut up
1 egg

Topping:

¼ cup brown sugar
2 tablespoons flour
2 tablespoons butter, cut up

Directions:

1. Mix sugar, flour, butter, and egg. Do not whisk as hard as Nellie Monroe, who is always too eager and violent.

2. Add rhubarb and let stand while preparing top and bottom piecrusts. You may not have my recipe because you must get your own, lazy English cook.

3. Line a pie pan with your crust, not mine. Pour in rhubarb mixture and cover with topping. You should have made that already. Pay attention.

4. Brush the top crust with a bit of milk. Sprinkle a little sugar but do not be wasteful. This will be difficult for you because you are English.

5. Bake the pie for one hour at 350 degrees Fahrenheit. It would be best to use that hour in a hardworking way, not in the frittering ways of Nellie Monroe. I will leave this to your decision, but I do not maintain high expectations.

A FINAL WORD FROM AMOS SHETLER,
FORMERLY OF THE OHIO OLD ORDER AMISH

Dear Most Gracious Reader,

Hello and what's up. My name is Amos Shetler, and I know that you have read a story about my life by Nellie Monroe, the girl with large hair who hits hard. First, I want to thank you for reading that book because it takes seriously patience to listen to Nellie for that long.

Number two, it is my desire to correct the mistakes of the manuscript. This most important mistake is that I am "not particularly tall" (chapter 19). I am, in real life, over five feet, eleven and three-quarters. And so it is painfully obvious that I am tall and very handsome. Plus, I am loyal to use much Electrify Pomade. This also adds to my height.

Also, I am a great dancer.

Thank you for the support. You are awesome!

Amos Shetler

440.555.0129

email: amosthestallion@nonmish.com